"Are you going ⟨...⟩ ⟨...⟩e okay?"

Reed's voice oozed ⟨...⟩
understanding. "D⟨...⟩
over there?"

Marina sighed. Of c⟨...⟩
okay. The eagerness ⟨...⟩ ⟨...⟩ough her
at his offer to come over was downright
embarrassing. Was she that eager to see
Reed at eleven o'clock at night?

"Marina?" The concern and caring in his
voice was like a mental caress.

"I—I'm fine," she managed. "I just needed
to talk."

"So I'll see you in the morning?"

"Yeah," she answered. "Have a good
night."

After he hung up, Marina prised the
phone from her ear and placed it back
on the cradle. Covering her eyes with her
fingers she moaned aloud, "What is wrong
with me?"

Later, as she climbed between the sheets,
the answer was all too obvious. She was
falling for Reed Crawford…again.

Available in May 2008 from Mills & Boon® Intrigue

A Serial Affair
NATALIE DUNBAR

MILLS & BOON
Pure reading pleasure

First published in Great Britain 2008
by Harlequin Mills & Boon Limited,
Eton House, 18-24 Paradise Road, Richmond, Surrey TW9 1SR

ISBN: 978 0 263 85960 7

46-0508

Harlequin Mills & Boon policy is to use papers that are natural, renewable and recyclable products and made from wood grown in sustainable forests. The logging and manufacturing processes conform to the legal environmental regulations of the country of origin.

Printed and bound in Spain
by Litografia Rosés S.A., Barcelona

Acknowledgements:

I want to thank my husband, Chet, and my boys
for all their love and support while I took time
away from them to write this book, was irritable
when the muse quit working, and didn't get to
things as planned.

Dedication:

This book is dedicated to the women who want
to have it all: good man, exciting job, love, family
and a good career. See it, believe it, then strive
to achieve it.

NATALIE DUNBAR

believes that a woman can do anything she sets
her mind to. To date, she has met her personal
goals of becoming an electrical engineer working
in the field, obtaining her master's degree in
business administration and getting published.
Happily married to her school sweetheart, she
lives in the Detroit area with him and their two
boys.

Dear Reader,

If you read a lot of thrillers and romantic suspense, you've probably noticed that there is no end to the women-in-jeopardy theme, or books where the serial killer is targeting women. This story was born out of the thought: How about a book where the killer is targeting men for a change?

This is my first Mills & Boon Romantic Suspense novel, and the tone and focus is very different from the other books I've written. I hope you enjoy *A Serial Affair*. Feel free to write to me about it at Natalie@nataliedunbar.com.

Natalie Dunbar

Prologue

Out by the pool, Elliot Washington sipped his mixed drink and grinned in anticipation of a night of hot sex. Clad only in a pair of swim trunks, he relaxed on a chaise longue. There wouldn't be many more nights like this because he would be getting married soon. Once the honeymoon phase with his blue-blooded bride was over, he'd be back in business, though.

He glanced at his watch. It was getting pretty late. He was used to getting what he wanted when he wanted it and that was a lot sooner than this. How long was he going to have to wait for satisfaction? "What's going on?" he asked his companion.

The words that came out of his mouth bore no resemblance to those he'd formed in his mind. He felt weird.

His gaze fell on the glass in his hand. A third of his Zombie remained. The glass on the table was empty. He could usually drink at least four before he flew this high.

His companion removed the glass from Elliot's numb fingers with a gloved hand and placed it on the table beside the other. Then his companion leaned over him, the long blond hair brushing Elliot's chest and stomach, tickling him. There was something distorted about his view of his surroundings and his companion, but he couldn't quite grasp what it was. Elliot gazed around him, enjoying the air of unreality. Then he saw the wicked-looking knife in his companion's hand.

"This is for all of us, for what you did. You see, you didn't really get away with it."

The words fell on Elliot's ears like a benediction.

The knife rose.

Gasping, Elliot tried to scream, to get away, anything but keep his body frozen to the chair. A whimper escaped his lips as the knife fell again and again....

Chapter 1

The whites of Marina Santos' mahogany-brown eyes shone bright in the bathroom mirror as she skillfully thickened her lashes with mascara. Quickly lining her lids, she filled in her eyebrows. Grumbling in frustration, she gave her thick hair one last impatient brush. Why hadn't she been blessed with easy-care hair like her cousins Janisa and Carmen? Maybe her hair would be easier to manage with a permanent.

Her full, berry-colored lips twisted ruefully. With the dense, moisture-laden July air, her shoulder-length hair would be even thicker before she got to work. She would have pulled it back, but she hated the drab, toned-down, buttoned-up look that most sported at her job. Wearing her hair down was one of the small ways she rebelled.

Straightening the casual navy pantsuit that she'd brightened with a multicolored camisole, she inserted a pair of ruby studs into her ears. In the background she could hear the Channel 9 news. Brushing lint off one sleeve of her jacket, she froze as she listened.

"Early this morning the body of twenty-six year-old Elliot Washington was found floating in the pool at the Hartford Hotel. The family has been notified. The cause of death has not been determined and police are not releasing details, but there are several reports that the body had been mutilated.

Washington was last seen partying with friends on the North End last night. You may recall that Washington was a close friend of Mayor Dansinger's daughter, Jade. He was a press favorite at several events featuring the mayor and his family.

Police are asking that anyone with information that might lead to an arrest contact them."

Marina stepped out of the bathroom in her low-heeled sensible shoes in time to see a television screen close-up of a tall blond man shown with the mayor's daughter. She recognized him from stories she'd seen on television and in the newspapers. A stockbroker, he was young, good-looking, and known to be a bit wild. Washington appeared often on the arm of the mayor's daughter and many speculated that things might have been heating up.

Eyes narrowing, Marina reached for her purse. Working under Lowell Talbot, the FBI's violent crimes expert, had so honed her instincts that she'd never look at life the way she used to. Now she saw patterns in everything. Leaping in anticipation of a new puzzle, the analytical part of her brain took in the news information, dissected it and searched for comparisons with things she'd seen and heard.

Reaching back in her memory, she recalled reading about a similar homicide several months ago. Hadn't there been another young man found dead and mutilated? *Yeah.* They'd found his mutilated body in a stall at Union Station. And she was betting that he hadn't been the first. It usually took three similarly patterned murders before a murderer was considered a serial killer. Could Chicago have a serial killer on the loose?

Washington's body had been mutilated, according to the reporter. Just what did they mean by "mutilated"? Working with Talbot she'd seen it all. Murder and mutilation were disturbing enough, but in general the damage was more visceral when a serial killer was involved. The victims were usually women. That made the possibilities in this instance even more intriguing. If her instincts were on target, this time a group of men was in danger.

Settling the strap of the purse on her shoulder and palming her car keys, she exited the front door of her remodeled brownstone. With the alarm set, she care-fully locked the door. She took the steps in brilliant sunlight, then opened the door of her red sports car, at which point she allowed herself to wonder. Has anyone else even noticed the two murders enough to tie them together? Of course, the Chicago Police Department had noticed, but that wouldn't be on the news. Getting the local population all excited with the news wouldn't be smart anyway.

Settling on the seat and buckling the safety belt, she savored the sound of the engine roaring to life, then took off in a squeal of tires.

By the time she'd parked her car and made it to her office at the National Center for the Analysis of Violent Crime, she knew something was up. Everyone seemed unusually busy as she'd passed on her way to her cubicle.

Scanning the office, she still didn't have a clue what was up. Some of her co-workers had been distant ever since she'd landed a promotion in the afterglow of helping Lowell Talbot solve a high-profile murder case. Marina straightened her shoulders. She'd earned that promotion and she'd be damned if she'd apologize for it.

Her boss's young blond secretary, Ilene, was hover-ing near her desk.

Marina checked her watch. She was still fifteen minutes early. She slowed her stride, sparing her boss's office a quick, surreptitious glance. The door was closed.

Marina greeted Ilene as she began to put her things in her desk.

"Keep the jacket on. Spaulding wants to see you in his office as soon as you get settled," Ilene announced.

Marina looked up from locking her purse in the bottom drawer. "What's going on?"

Ilene shrugged, her expression giving discreet evidence of the battle within her. She didn't like Marina, but was still the kind of person who enjoyed knowing things others didn't and controlling the flow of information. "I think you're going to get a new assignment," she admitted.

"Tell me something I don't know," Marina prompted, slanting her a glance.

Nostrils flaring, Ilene's gaze flicked over her. "This one is big. You'll either fall on your face or prove you deserved that promotion."

"I got the promotion because I've already more than proved myself, but I'm down for a new assignment." Marina straightened, ready to squash any smart-assed comment Ilene might make. Still, she swallowed at the smirk on Ilene's face.

"We'll see." Turning abruptly, Ilene headed back to her desk.

Marina hesitated, torn between rushing into her boss's office to hear the news as soon as possible and enjoying the last minute of peace she was likely to get for some time. She opted for the momentary peace and headed for the coffee room with her cup. Three gulps of hot coffee later she knocked at her boss's door.

"Santos!" Ross Spaulding called, beckoning her into the room, "I've been waiting for you."

Inclining her head in acknowledgment, she took a seat at his conference table. "What is it, sir?"

"We got a call from the mayor's office this morning," he announced. "Dansinger is asking us to work with the Chicago Police Department on a special task force."

"And how does Chicago's finest feel about us encroaching on their territory?" she quipped.

"Damn lucky for a change!" Spaulding grinned almost affably. "With the economy being so rough right now, crime has almost doubled in Chicago. The C.P.D. has got just about all they can handle." The smile faded as he eyed her critically. "Been paying attention to the news lately?"

"What kind of violent crime are we talking?" she asked.

"You're the expert. What do you think? Why do you think you're sitting in the hot seat?" he countered.

Her eyes widened. She hadn't wanted to draw conclusions since the request had come from the mayor's office and she'd been assigned the case, but deep in her gut she knew. "Are we talking Elliot Washington and the other man being found dead, their bodies mutilated, within a four- or five-month period?"

"Bingo." Spaulding weighed her with his eyes. She'd gotten points for that answer. "Washington's death has the mayor's family pretty upset. Jade Dansinger thought she was in love with him apparently."

"Was there another incident, another body?" she asked.

Spaulding's beefy fist choked the life out of an ink pen as his head inclined in answer to her question. "You'll work with one of their homicide lieutenants and you'll have resources available from the Chicago Police Department and the FBI. I don't have to tell you how important this case is for us, and to you and your career?"

"No, sir. I will find the killer." Marina spoke with cool confidence but inside she was bouncing off the walls with nervous excitement. Spaulding hadn't promoted her to his section. She'd been promoted and dumped on him by his management. Since then, they'd both been trying to make the best of it. Her fingers tightened on the edges of the chair beneath the table.

He made a rough grinding sound in the back of his throat. "I've had agents waste valuable time and taxpayer dollars wrestling with the C.P.D. over jurisdictional issues and one-upmanship. Don't even think of letting the fact that you'll be working with the C.P.D. keep you from solving this case as soon as possible, understand?"

"Yes, sir. I can work with them," she said quickly, hoping her new partner wouldn't be a complete ass.

Spaulding's piercing gaze sized her up once more. He nodded as if she'd passed some test. "You're due at the Twenty-fourth District Town Hall Station on Halstead at ten-thirty, so get moving. Talbot wants you to check in with him before you leave."

Marina thanked him and left the office. Outside, she let herself breathe. She could do this. She would do this. The prospect actually excited her.

At his desk in the Homicide Unit, finishing some paperwork, Lieutenant Reed Crawford's jaw clenched, as his temper shot up like a rocket. Two desks over, Lieutenant Warwick was meeting with a community activist and a local reporter about the high-profile murder of one of the Chicago Bears' assistant coaches. Evidently, there was going to be an article in the paper. That didn't bother him so much. What burned Reed the most was that somehow Warwick had scooped him again by getting the assignment from Shepherd. When had that happened? Better yet, how?

If it was just about the work, he could deal with it, but he and Warwick were the top candidates for a promotion. If Reed just took it as the luck of the draw, then in a few months he'd probably be standing on the sidelines as Warwick accepted the promotion they'd both been pushing for. Reed was determined to use all his skills and abilities to serve the community and lead the department to greater glory in its war against crime.

After postponing his dreams of becoming an FBI agent to stick close to home to help care for his ailing mother, he'd discovered that he really liked police work. The competition for the promotions was so heated and contentious he'd learned to get in line early and make sure the folks in the head shed knew just who he was.

Reed stood, placing the reports he'd been finishing back into folders and pushing the folders into a neat pile. He headed for the captain's office, more than aware that it was time to look out for his own interests. He'd made lieutenant on his own and he'd get the next promotion the same way.

Ean Shepherd was at his desk, chomping on an unlit cigar. Reed knew it was a bad sign. Shepherd had been trying to stop smoking all year. For the most part, he'd succeeded, but when stressed or under pressure Shepherd went back to chomping. The one concession was that most of the time it stayed unlit. "What do you want, Crawford?" he barked, spotting Reed in the doorway.

Having worked for Shepherd for two years, Reed immediately realized that he should have waited to approach the man. "I wanted to talk assignments, but if this is a bad time…"

"It ain't gonna get any better," Shepherd snapped. "From the mayor's office to the brass, I've had my ass chewed so many times today it's medium rare. You wait much longer I won't have any ass left, so get in here."

Stepping into the office and closing the door, Reed dropped down into the seat in front of the desk.

"So what's got your jaw so tight?"

"Warwick's working the Chicago Bears' case and I'm still off in the weeds with a desk full of crap. Captain, I want that promotion. I need an assignment that will give me some of the same exposure and experience as he's getting."

Shepherd eyed him speculatively. Then he nodded. "Mmm-hmm." A grin formed on both sides of the cigar in Shepherd's mouth. "Crawford, I've got just the job for you."

This was too easy. The sudden change in the captain made Reed do a double take. "Sir?"

Shepherd threw the soggy cigar into the trash can and tilted back in his chair. "One of the reasons they've been raining down the love on me is that it looks like we've got a serial killer on our hands. With the caseload we've got right now, I don't have any of my most experienced guys available to take it, but the mayor and the chief of police want a task force to take it on now. That's where you come in, Crawford. The mayor's already asked the FBI to help us out. They're providing an agent who's also a violent crimes expert. You'll have department resources and those of the National Center for the Analysis of Violent Crime—NCAVC—and the Violent Criminal Apprehension Program—VICAP—behind you. That's why I can put you on this task force so that you can get the experience and a bit of the limelight. What do you think?"

Reed had never had an opportunity to work with the FBI, but knew from some of his co-workers that the agents could be an arrogant lot. On the other hand, he did know one agent, Marina Santos, who was smart, fiery and hot, and as far as you could get from arrogant. They'd almost had a thing until she'd drop-kicked him in favor of a Puerto Rican guy.

As the silence grew uncomfortably long, he pushed his thoughts past Marina. This was an opportunity he couldn't afford to pass up. Besides, what were the chances of Marina, out of all the agents working crime in the local office, being assigned to work the task force with him? He spoke confidently. "I want to take on the assignment, sir. I think I could do us proud."

Captain Shepherd flashed him an evil grin and tapped his fingers on the oak desk. "You'd better. I want you to catch this killer before he or she kills again. And don't get tight-assed about working with the Feds. Some of them are okay guys and gals."

Reed nodded. "Yes, sir. Can you give me some detail on this serial killer case?"

"Someone's out there killing young men and mutilating the bodies. We've got two bodies identified right now and suspect there's more. The latest victim was Elliot Washington, a friend of the mayor's daughter. His body was found this morning floating in the pool over at the Hartford Hotel. Both men were in their mid to late twenties. Both had been stabbed and castrated."

Ouch! Reed swallowed, shifting uncomfortably in his seat. This was definitely an interesting case. He could only imagine the motivation behind someone taking the time to murder *and* castrate someone.

The captain studied him, looking for a sign of weakness. "Still think you can do this task force deal?"

Reed nodded. "Yes, sir. I'm ready to roll on it. Just give me the names and I'll pull the files."

"No need for that." The captain handed him two folders. The one on top had Washington's name on it. "You can do a search on the system to see if you can come up with the others."

"Thank you." Reed accepted the files and rose.

"One other thing, Crawford. Since Farrell is still in

the hospital, you can use his office as the task force office for now. I had Betty put away his things."

Thanking him again, Reed got out of his office. He was excited at the prospect of putting a face to whoever killed Washington and the other guy, and catching the killer before he could kill again. The only potential bug on his butt was the FBI agent he'd have to work with. He'd heard enough stories to make his hands curl into fists.

On the way back to his desk Reed tried to relax. If the FBI sent a snot-nosed, tight-assed wonder boy, he'd just have to make him see the light. He could do that, couldn't he? He'd show him that the C.P.D. was truly a world-class team.

Chapter 2

Marina drove over to the Twenty-fourth District Town Hall Station on Halstead and sweet-talked the guard into letting her park in the police lot. She could have gone inside first, shown her badge and gotten a permit, but there was nowhere close to park and she wasn't taking any chances with someone trying to steal her sports car. That was her baby.

Inside the station, she straightened her shoulders, flashed her badge at the officer on the desk and informed him that she had arrived for the task force.

He stared at her, obviously having a hard time lifting his gaze above her breasts. Marina's breasts were 38Ds, so she got that a lot, but it didn't mean she had to like the extra attention. "Officer, is there a problem?" she asked, hardening her tone.

He immediately lifted his gaze to make eye contact. "No. No, ma'am, no problem." Then he checked a list and directed her to a room around the corner and across the hall.

Deeper into what she'd jokingly named the Den of Testosterone, Marina peered into the small, smoked-glass window on the office where she'd been directed. With his back to her, a caramel-skinned man with a head full of thick dark hair sat at a desk, his head bent over a file. She guessed that he was her new partner on the task force, already hard at work. She fleetingly thought those wide muscular shoulders and well-shaped head looked familiar. She opened the door and stepped in, dragging her laptop in the rolling case behind her. "Good morning, I'm Marina Santos and I've been assigned to the task force."

At the sound of her voice he lifted his head and turned around, recognizing her instantly. "Marina?"

"Reed?" Forcing air through her lungs, Marina felt like she'd stepped through a time warp. She gazed into those golden-brown eyes, aware that Reed Crawford was as surprised but not particularly as happy to see her. She knew him, had gone to college with him, even kissed that full mouth a time or two. She'd also been accepted at the FBI academy along with him, but he'd had to opt out due to his mother's illness.

Other than deciding not to make him a boyfriend

last year, what had she done to deserve that look? If she hadn't known better, she'd have said it hurt her feelings. She still saw him every other month at a gathering of friends and he always seemed as friendly as ever.

"So you're the violent crime expert the FBI's assigned to the task force?" he asked, as if he still wasn't quite ready to believe it.

"That's what I just said," she confirmed a bit too brightly as she pulled out the chair at the desk next to his.

"So, how've you been?" he asked, recovering quickly.

"I'm fine." She turned to confront him. "But you look…disappointed. Why?"

Golden-brown eyes made serious contact with hers. She experienced a physical jolt that she felt all over, almost as if she'd been pushed by all the energy in that gaze. Reed had depths she'd never taken the time to explore.

"To be frank, I'm not disappointed," he began with a glint of amusement in his eyes, "but I was sort of expecting one of the guys, an up-and-coming special agent?"

Marina wasn't going to drop the subject. "You already know I got promoted recently, but I've still got a ways to go. You got everything right except the guy part," she pressed.

His gaze assessed her, taking her in as a whole. Then he nodded. "Yeah, right. If you're wondering if I have a problem with you working on this task force because you're female or because we're friends, forget it. Just don't expect me to kiss your ass. Okay?"

"Okay, but don't be surprised if you piss me off and I tell you to kiss my ass anyway." Marina grinned.

Reed chuckled, shaking his head.

She'd made her point, he'd put her in her place and she'd managed a good comeback. "How's Trudy?" Marina asked, her tone softening.

Something in his posture eased. "Ma's doing a lot better. She's fine as long as we keep taking care of her. Ron and I take turns fixing her meals, testing her blood sugar and giving her the medication and shots. She goes to an activity center during the day where she's taking a couple of classes." Reed rocked his chair back and forth. "You know, she asks about you all the time."

"Really? What do you tell her?" Her question hung on the air for several moments while she imagined several nasty explanations he could have used.

His expression was calm, but there was a darkness in his eyes that made her cringe and feel guilty. Reed answered in an easy tone did not match what she saw in his eyes. "I've told her that you've moved on, and that you've been busy with your career. She wants to see you, so she can congratulate you on your promotion."

Marina was almost certain that he was still angry with her about the way she'd ended things. She shouldn't care, *but she did.* Whether she and Reed ever got together as a couple or not, she genuinely liked him as a person. He could be provocative and mysterious, and irritating, but he was still a genuinely nice guy that she liked to be around.

"I'll have to drop by to see her sometime," she mumbled.

He was silent when he shot her a look of disbelief. "And what's Javier up to?" he asked, referring to her dad.

"Javier is Javier." She sighed dramatically, not wanting go into the details of how her amorous father was inexplicably without a love interest for the first time in years. He had been driving Marina crazy with his determination to spend more time with her. She abruptly changed the subject. "Where's the rest of the team hiding out?"

"I am the rest of the team." He watched her take the computer out of her case and set it on the desk. Then he showed her the socket to plug in her power cord. "You know I work the Homicide Unit and I'm good. I have access to their resources and anything the C.P.D. has to offer. Where's the rest of your FBI team?"

This time she smiled. "You're looking at it. I've got access to the National Center for the Analysis of Violent Crime database and the VICAP and anything else we'll need from the FBI."

"We've got everything we need to bring down the killer." Reed returned the smile and this time it was close to the charming, earnest one she was used to seeing. "If we really push it, maybe we can chase the killer down before the trail grows cold. We need to leave in about thirty minutes. Jade Dansinger was too upset to talk to homicide detectives early this morning. I've been calling the mayor's mansion to set up another interview. The okay came just a few minutes ago. We need to talk to her and her friends about last night and anything they may have seen or heard. I've already lined up interviews with several of her and Washington's friends."

Marina nodded. "How about the staff at the hotel?" she asked.

"Third-shift detectives on the scene this morning interviewed them."

Hope surged within Marina that they would have another piece of the puzzle. "Did anyone see anything?"

"Not really. They knew that Washington was out at the pool with someone, but no one bothered to look. Apparently, Jade and Elliot often took late-night skinny-dips and paid the staff to give them their privacy. There's actually a room at the back of the hotel with its own private pool."

Marina expelled a puff of air. "So do they at least know if Washington was out there with a woman?"

Reed shook his head. "No. No one saw or heard a thing. Washington must not have cried out or struggled enough to draw attention."

Marina considered his statement. "Maybe he couldn't. Maybe the first blow incapacitated him or he was already pretty much out of it. I hope they took samples of his blood."

Spearing her with a glance, Reed said, "Bring that nose down a bit. Our crew is one of the best. They got the blood samples, some DNA from the scene and prints from the chair he'd been sitting in and the ones next to it. The forensic team is doing their thing. We should have all of the results in a few days."

Marina nodded. "I don't suppose anyone found the murder weapon?"

"You dream big, don't you?" Reed remarked.

"It was worth a try," she murmured, settling into her chair. "I'll just take a quick look at the files."

While Reed checked on the database search he'd initiated earlier, Marina set up her computer and opened a new spreadsheet. Then she got her first look at the files.

One file was that of Elliot Washington, the guy she'd heard about on the morning news. The other file was for the young man identified as twenty-five-year-old elementary school teacher, Colton Edwards. His body had been found in the middle of an empty stall at Union Station.

Working violent crime with Talbot, she'd learned the hard way that murder was never pretty. Mentally bracing herself, Marina went through the crime scene photos. Her stomach quivered.

Someone had stabbed Washington repeatedly and unmanned him with butcher-block precision. She hadn't heard that part on the news. Had Washington still been alive when his killer had done that? Marina hoped not because it seemed that the killer's need to punish and degrade had been strong. Her stomach threatened to heave.

Momentarily looking away, she found Reed watching her.

"Pretty graphic, huh?"

Marina nodded. "I've seen worse, but looking at this stuff never gets easier."

Reed's gaze dropped back to the screen. "No, it doesn't."

She pointed to the stack of pictures. "Just examining the way the bodies were maimed, it appears that we're dealing with a serial killer who's also a sexual predator. There are several famous serial killer cases where men and young boys were abducted, assaulted and brutalized, maimed and killed. Leaving the severed organs near the victim's body appears to be our killer's signature, as in actions he does above and beyond his mode of operation. If this is the case, then our killer will do this to all of the victims."

Reed secured Edwards' file and paged through to the selection of pictures. The wounds to his body and the gruesome removal and placement of the organs was similar to what had been done to Washington. His girlfriend, his mother and his fifth-grade class had been devastated. They'd written the heart-wrenching letters in the file to the detective handling the case.

Forcing herself to swallow against the dryness in her throat, Marina moved on.

In Washington's file she noted that he'd gone to her and Reed's alma mater, Merriwhether University of Chicago. He'd obtained a degree in business administration. On impulse she checked Edwards' file. Same college, only his degree was in education. Typing the information onto the new spreadsheet, she wondered if she'd already found the most important link. If so, did that mean that Reed qualified as a potential victim? At twenty-nine, he was a few years older than both men. Only time would tell if he, too, was in danger.

Reed checked his watch and stood. "We've got to get going."

Opting to leave her laptop locked in the task force office, because it could be intimidating to some witnesses and a chore to keep up with, Marina grabbed her purse and followed him out.

"Did you notice that both victims went to Merri-whether?" she asked as they got into an unmarked blue Crown Victoria.

"Yeah," Reed answered grudgingly as he backed out of the parking space and took off. "What's your point?"

"I know that you and a lot of people went to Merri-whether, but until we get more facts about this killer and how he's picking his victims, you should be careful."

"So you think I'm in danger?"

She didn't like the trace of amusement that crept into his voice. "Reed, this could be serious," she insisted, feeling like a teacher cautioning a child bent on ignoring reason. "You're only a couple of years older than Washington and Edwards."

"Fact, but what else do I have in common with them?"

Marina's teeth kneaded her bottom lip. "That's the ten-million-dollar question."

With a slight shrug, he accelerated and entered the

freeway. "I don't remember seeing them on campus and I never met either of them."

He appeared to be dismissing her arguments. Folding her arms in front of her, she threw him annoyed glance.

Those impossibly long lashes of his were still as he concentrated on the road.

Marina turned to stare out the window at the Chicago countryside. Were all men so arrogant or just the ones she knew?

"Of course I plan to watch myself and stay on guard," he said, breaking the sudden silence.

Turning from the window, she met his amused glance.

"Don't take yourself so seriously," he said. "The work we do can be depressing enough."

"Don't *you* try to diminish the importance of what's going on here," she replied without a trace of amusement. "I'd hate to lose you as a member of this task force."

"Is that all?" he asked softly.

Of course it wasn't all. He was still her friend and she didn't want to lose him. "Well, you've been my friend for how long?" she asked, making eye contact and letting her voice trail off. "I'd hate to lose you period."

Something in his rapt gaze made her swallow reflexively. Was he trying to make her say that she still had feelings for him? She did, but they were tangled in a maze of emotions, thoughts and feelings resulting from the choice she'd made. Being alone with him for the first time in ages forced her to see him in a new light and it made her uncomfortable.

She was relieved when he turned his attention back to the road. Opening some of the files they'd brought along, she immersed herself in the notes the third shift detectives had made while interviewing the hotel staff.

At the mayor's home, they flashed their badges and were shown to a library filled with couches and chairs, a large cherry desk and antique shelves of leather-bound books. Marina and Reed took seats in the flower-patterned armchairs in front of the bay window. Sunlight filtered in, warming the air-conditioned room.

The staff informed them that the mayor was away on business, but due back soon, and that Mrs. Dansinger and Jade would be in momentarily. Then they offered tea. Translating that to mean that Jade would be a while, Marina accepted a cup.

Ten minutes later, Jade Dansinger and her mother, Laura, entered the library. Poor Jade's eyes were red and swollen, her aquiline nose pinched and flushed. She hadn't bothered with makeup. The black silk pantsuit did nothing for her white complexion and slim frame. Her eyes were pale blue. A fall of baby-fine, platinum-blond hair covered her face when she took a seat on the couch next to her mother. Her collagen-filled lips quivered as she answered their questions.

Elliot Washington had taken a call on his cell phone and left the party on the North End at about midnight to meet a friend. He'd told Jade that it was part of the big surprise he was planning for her and had insisted on going alone. He'd driven himself in his Jag. Marina made a note to look at the cell phone records C.P.D. had undoubtedly subpoenaed.

"Did Elliot seem upset or worried?" Reed asked, scribbling in his notebook.

"No, he was happy," Jade answered in a voice clogged with tears.

"Did he say or give you the name of the friend he was meeting?" Reed continued.

"No."

Marina added a question of her own. "Do you know if he was meeting a male or female friend?"

The mayor's wife shot Marina a warning glance. Laura Dansinger was fiercely protective of her family. She handled the police and press with an iron hand.

Jade's eyes widened with shock and outrage. "He wasn't meeting another woman, if that's what you mean! He wasn't cheating on me."

With a surreptitious glance at the others in the room, Marina noted that none of their faces reflected the same outrage. Most showed pity. Laura Dansinger's chin dropped. She slowly brought it back up, meeting Marina's gaze with pure strength of will.

"We were unofficially engaged," Jade continued, showing them the four-carat diamond ring on her finger. "Daddy was going to announce it this week and Elliot was working on a surprise for me."

"But you don't really know who he met, do you?" Reed interjected calmly.

Jade's voice cracked. "No."

"Did he often spend the night at the Hartford Hotel?" Marina asked carefully.

Dabbing at her eyes, Jade took her time answering. "We…we went for lunch sometimes and after parties," she admitted in a low voice.

Evening haven and afternoon delight? This more or less had been verified by some of the hotel staff's statements to the police. Marina made a few notes in the little book she kept in her purse and kept her expression bland.

Reed looked up from his notes. "When he left the party, did you notice anyone else leaving?"

Jade shook her head negatively. "No."

"Do you know if he'd received any threatening notes or letters?" Reed asked.

"No. Everyone liked him." More tears fell from Jade's eyes. She wiped at them with a tissue.

Marina chewed the top of her pen. "We need a list of all his friends and ex-girlfriends."

Jade's chin came up, her lips quivering again. She'd obviously been hiding something. She chose her words carefully. "His ex-girlfriend was Lissa Rawlins and he dropped her when he met me. She…she was angry at first, but I think she got over it."

Nodding carefully, Marina noted it. Then she urged Jade to list the names of Elliot's friends and note which friends had been at the party. As she and Reed finished the interview, she asked if Elliot had known Colton Edwards. Jade did not recognize the name, but added that Edwards could have worked at Quarter Financial with Elliot or attended MUC with him.

Respectfully reserving the right to return with more questions if necessary, Reed and Marina left the mayor's mansion.

In the interest of getting as much done as possible, they stopped to pick up fast-food sandwiches on the way to their next interview. Eating as they traveled, they arrived at the apartment of Elliot's best friend, Josh Jones, in Rogers Park.

Jones was obviously grief-stricken about the death of his friend. Through questioning, he basically confirmed the things Jade told them, except he thought they should check the alibi for Elliot's ex-girlfriend, Lissa. When Elliot dropped her for Jade, Lissa'd had a hard time accepting it and had been angry enough to stalk him and cause a scene in several restaurants and clubs. When asked about Elliot's late-night meeting, Jones told them that Elliot sometimes met and slept with other women on the side, and that everyone but Jade knew that was the reason he'd left the party early. Jones knew nothing about the woman he assumed Elliot went to meet.

Marina and Reed left Jones' apartment and hurried to the last-known address for Lissa Rawlins. It was a condo near Grant Park. Flashing their badges, they got past the front desk guard. According to the guard and the sign on the mailbox in the lobby, it was still Lissa's place, but no one answered the bell or the phone number Jones had given them. On the way over Reed had checked with Homicide, and they had not been able to talk to Lissa, either. Marina and Reed decided they would call back in the morning.

Heading for the office, Reed and Marina agreed to call it a day. Halfway there, Marina's stomach growled so mournfully that she turned her head in embarrassment.

On the other side of the car Reed chuckled. "Want me to stop for some carry-out?"

"I would," she replied regretfully, "but I promised to have dinner with Dad tonight.

"Father, daughter dinner, huh?" Reed grinned.

"Yeah. He insisted, and he's been a little weird lately."

Reed turned his head to make momentary eye contact. "You don't think he's sick?"

"I hope not." Marina considered the thought and dismissed it. Her father was a big baby. If he were sick, she'd know it because for most of her twenty-eight years she'd been his number-one choice for unofficial nurse. "Nah, he seems to be having some sort of midlife crisis."

"Again?"

Something in Reed's tone made her want to defend her father. He could be very dramatic and quite emotional, but she never doubted his love or that he had her best interests at heart. "Okay, Reed. Cut him some slack. He hit his fiftieth birthday in January and has been trying to fight getting older every step of the way."

Reed simply laughed, a warm, rumbling sound that made her smile in return.

"All right, now, you'll get there someday yourself," she warned.

"Lord, I hope so." Reed maneuvered the car around a corner. "I plan to have it all by then."

"And what does having it all mean for you these days?" she asked, venturing deeper into the personal without thinking.

"Smart, hot-looking, sex freak of a wife who's crazy about me, a couple of kids, big house in the burbs, a job as captain, and a Jag."

"You don't ask for much, do you?" she quipped.

"Hey, I'm working on it. What about you?"

Marina clasped her hands behind her head. "Tall, good-looking hunk of a husband who treats me like a queen and knows how to admit when he's wrong, a couple of kids, a house that we love, a challenging job, the latest Mustang…"

They were at the red light near the station. Reed turned to face her. She sensed seriousness beneath his light tone. "You've got the sports car and the job. How are you coming on the rest?"

Marina forced a smile. "Now I've got to find the man, then work on the house and kids."

They flashed their badges as he drove through the gate into the station lot. He spoke in an even tone. "What happened to Emilio?"

She fought an unreasonable wave of guilt. She'd really made a mess of ending things with Reed by letting things simmer between them too long. Ending the romance between them had been difficult. All was fair in love and war, wasn't it? She answered him in a casual tone. "Emilio was a nice guy, but it didn't work out."

Reed parked the car. He took the key out of the ignition and faced her. Most of the warmth had faded from his expression. "That's too bad."

"Yes, it is," she replied, pushing back with her tone. The sudden distance between them made Marina feel as if she'd been slapped. There'd been an unsaid criticism in his expression and his voice. There'd been a hint of "you made your bed now lie in it" in his tone, too. That made her mad. Reed had no right to judge her or her actions. If his shorts were still twisted over what had happened in the past, it was too damned bad.

Snapping her mouth shut, she got out of the car. "See you tomorrow," she called over her shoulder. He replied, but she really didn't hear it because she was too busy walking to her car and fuming.

Driving home she reflected on her first day on the assignment and hoped that past history wasn't going to make Reed a pain in the ass to work with. Finding the serial killer would be difficult enough.

She thought about poor Jade and then the unlucky Elliot Washington. He'd obviously chosen the wrong woman to cheat with. Had Elliot's ex, Lissa, been that woman? Marina was looking forward to their talk with Lissa Rawlins.

Chapter 3

Marina Santos always managed to push Reed's buttons whether she wanted to or not. Wound up from his first day on the task force, and more than a little out of sorts from seeing Marina and trying to adjust to working with her, Reed grabbed a quick hot dog on a bun covered with chili gravy and onions at his favorite Coney Island restaurant. He drove around the city until he reached one of his favorite spots, the Xsport Fitness Gym. He worked out and pumped iron until most of the restless feeling disappeared.

Instead of heading home this time, Reed turned his truck onto his mother's street. It wasn't his evening to take care of her, but he was close enough to stop and check on her. Her blood sugar levels had been fluctuating, her blood pressure was high, and she'd seemed overtired the last couple of days. The area's streetlights were out again. Porch lights shone like an oasis on several neighborhood homes, but they did little to dispel the gathering darkness. The small one- and two-story brick structures were old and worn.

Most of the older inhabitants had already given up the warm evening air for the relative safety and security found inside their homes. Like his mother, Trudy, they were clinging to the homes they loved come hell or high water.

Here and there, youths sat on porches or stood in groups talking. The old neighborhood was rundown and becoming dangerous for those unable to hold their own against the local toughs and predators looking for victims.

Reed parked the truck in front of his mother's house. The porch light was off but a warm glow around the edges of the blinds indicated that his mother was still up and about.

Peering around the quiet block, he got out of the truck. A warm evening breeze enveloped him. Something moved in the dark. Reed froze. His hand moved close to the Glock pistol he wore strapped at his waist. Innate caution and the desire not to hurt anyone unless it became absolutely necessary kept him from drawing the pistol.

Reed stood listening to the darkness. Nothing but the wind. He studied the surrounding trees and bushes, looking for movement. Nothing. Still his instincts told him that someone was hiding in the darkness, watching him. Instinct had saved his life more times than he cared to remember.

Fleetingly, he thought about being stalked. He wasn't the kind of man who saw menace everywhere. In the truck earlier, he'd dismissed Marina's suggestion that he could be in danger from the serial killer because the profile was still too general, but the possibility remained. He thought of Elliot Washington and Colton Edwards. Maybe someone had stalked and watched them in the dark before moving in close to viciously attack them.

Dismissing the thought, Reed stepped around the side of the truck. It was more likely that a druggie or neighborhood tough was lurking in the bushes, hoping to mug him. "Police officer. Who's there?" he called into the dark.

Footsteps echoed on the sidewalk and changed to the muffled sound of someone running across the grass. The sound of breaking glass fractured the relative silence. His pulse raced. Reed drew the high-powered flashlight from his pocket and switched it on. Illuminating the trees, bushes and sidewalk, he satisfied himself that no one hid nearby. Walking up the driveway, he headed for the back of the house to check for broken glass.

Easing between his mother's house and the one next door, he was glad for the absence of trees and bushes to hide an attacker. Behind the house, broken bottle glass littered the area near the trash. He guessed that someone had thrown the bottle to attract his attention.

Shining his light over the small garage and the few trees in his mother's yard and the yards on either side of her, he saw nothing out of the ordinary. "Damn fool kids," he muttered under his breath as he returned to the front. He would sweep up the glass tomorrow when it was daylight.

Warm light and cooler air hit him in the face as he used his keys to open the security door and enter the house. Inside, Trudy Crawford sat at her desktop computer under a floodlight in a corner of her living room.

Golden-brown eyes mirrored his. Seeing him, her mouth broke into a smile. "Hey, Be-be," she said pleasantly as she pulled the reading glasses off her nose and laid them in front of the large magnifying screen on the desk. "What's up, Lieutenant?"

She was so proud of him that she never tired of calling him that. "Just you, Mom," he said with a smile of his own. "How are you feeling?"

"I'm okay," she assured him. "I've got two wonderful sons who make sure I stay that way."

"What was your sugar level?"

"Four hundred," she answered, looking properly chastened, "but I didn't eat anything that wasn't on the diet today. I even turned down the muffins in knitting class. I must be coming down with something."

"I hope not." Moving closer, he kissed her cheek and enjoyed the warm hug. As she released him, he took one look at the computer screen and burst into laughter. "Computer dating for seniors, Mom?"

"Why not?" she asked with a straight face. "I'm not looking to get married, but I could sure use some company. I don't remember the last time I had a date."

"I take you out to dinner every week, Mom," he reminded her.

She gave him the look and deepened her tone. "And you're my son. You're cute, but you don't count, Be-be."

He studied the questionnaire she'd been filling out. He didn't like the idea of his mother dating someone off the Internet. He knew that all sorts of predators lurked there, hidden behind their computers. Still, Trudy wasn't his child; she was his mother and would do as she pleased. "Don't give them any personal information."

"Of course not," she agreed readily, "And you'll probably want to personally meet and check out any of them before we go out, right?"

"For sure." Reed pulled a chair up next to her. "Why don't I help you with the form?"

"I'd love that." She patted his hand. "You sure you don't have a date or something better to do?"

"What could be better than you?"

Trudy grabbed his hand and shook it gently. "Don't try to play me, son, 'cause I've been played by the best of them and am still here to talk about it. Your heart ain't been into dating since you messed around with Marina and things fell apart. Let's talk about *your* social calendar."

"I've got a date with Sondra. We're going to dinner and the movies on Friday," he said as he started adding his mother's name to the computer form.

Trudy snorted. "Sondra does not count, and you know it. You're not interested in her."

Still typing, Reed bit back a smile. He'd never said anything, but his mother was right. "I got a new assignment today at work," he began, changing the subject.

An hour later he let himself out. He'd talked about the task force assignment but neglected to mention that Marina was the FBI agent he would be working with. In his mind he'd rationalized his omission because he didn't want to get his mother's hopes up. Both he and Marina had moved on. The uneasiness between them now was only due to both of them trying to figure out how to work with each other on a daily basis.

Outside the house he stepped into warm darkness once more. There was no one around. As he neared his Explorer Sportrac, he noticed that it was pitched at an odd angle. Whipping out his flashlight he examined the tires. The front tire on the driver's side had been slashed.

From time to time youths in the neighborhood vandalized property, but Reed seldom had a problem. He hoped there was no connection with his new assignment.

Angry, Reed surveyed the area once more, certain that someone was behind the curtains of a nearby house, laughing. The perpetrator was long gone. Opening the trunk, he took out his tire iron and jack, and got to work. He was going to have to be more cautious at work and during his time off. Hopefully this wasn't the start of something nasty.

* * *

Marina's dinner with her dad at the Italian restaurant was a dramatic affair. In between salad and lasagna, Javier, darkly handsome with just a touch of silver at his temples, was usually a very charming and talkative man. Tonight he punctuated the silences with soulful sighs. This unconscious habit was something he did when he was worried and wanted to discuss his concerns with her. Through conversation she usually got it out of him.

For some unfathomable reason she suspected that this was one time she should ignore the signals. When she could stand it no more, she fixed him with an exasperated gaze. "What? What is it, Dad? What's got you so stressed?"

He reached across the table to pat her hand. "Marina, you know you're my heart. Maybe I didn't always make the best example for you, but I always tried to do my best."

Cocking her head to the side, she gave him a puzzled look. "Sometimes you drive me crazy, but you're a wonderful dad. Have I ever complained?"

He shook his head. "No, but it's not your nature. I should have remarried after your mother died, let you see what it's like to have a mother around all the time instead of…all the girlfriends."

This time Marina sighed loudly. Her father was as amorous as they came. Simply put, he liked women, and age, beauty and intelligence were no barriers. One concession she appreciated was that he'd never dated any of her friends, but that hadn't dampened the interest of a determined few once they reached legal age. "Dad, where are you going with this?"

Javier gripped her hand. "*Chica,* is it my fault that you don't get married?"

"No." She eyed him as if he'd transformed into a three-legged chicken. "Uh—how'd you come up with that?"

"You and your cousins Janisa and Carmen, are all about the same age, but both of them are married. Carmen's little Chico has the birthday party this week. Janisa is expecting. But you, you are alone. You don't even have a boyfriend. Why not? I want you to be happy. And I can hardly wait for some grandchildren."

"You'll get grandchildren. One day," she added quickly. "What's the rush?"

"You're twenty-eight now. You don't have a long time to make babies."

Marina rolled her eyes. "Uh…thanks, Dad. Do you think I'm almost old enough to retire?"

Ignoring her comment, he thrust another question at her. "What happened to Emilio?"

"I told you. It didn't work out."

"But you liked him. *We liked him.*" Javier's tone deepened and he leaned forward, intent on pressing his point.

It had been a number of months since she'd sent Emilio on his way. Resenting her father's pushing him-self into her love life, Marina leaned forward, too. "Yes, I liked him, but I didn't *love* him and he wanted to get married."

"Then what about the other guy? Rich? Rod?"

"Reed," Marina corrected. "And don't tell me you liked him. I know better."

"He was okay," Javier corrected her gently. "But his Spanish wasn't that good and he didn't share the Puerto Rican heritage of our family."

"Mama was African-American," she stated flatly.

"Yes, *mija,* my daughter, I loved her very much. Why do you think no one has replaced her?"

"And her Spanish was good?" she asked, knowing the answer but wanting to hear him say more.

"Her Spanish was excellent. She tutored me in English."

"But she didn't share the Puerto Rican heritage," Marina noted, just to see what he'd say.

Javier's eyes lit up as he gazed inwardly. "To tell you the truth, I was so in love with Lily Ann Taylor, she could have been an alien and I would have followed her to the end of the universe."

"Oh, Dad." Marina gave his hand a squeeze. Hearing her dad talk about her mother often made her misty-eyed.

Javier lifted her hand and kissed it. "That's what I want for you, *mija,* a love so strong that nothing else matters."

"Maybe one day," she murmured, wishing she could get misty-eyed about a love of her own.

The waiter came and give them dessert menus. Marina studied hers, hoping her dad was through poking into her love life. She'd never experienced a love so strong that nothing else mattered, and couldn't even imagine that notion. The truth was that she'd never experienced love at all. What she'd had with Emilio had been a comfortable combination of lust and like with enthusiastic family approval on both sides.

"Tell me about your job," her father said, starting a welcome new thread of conversation. "What's going on with that?"

Marina told him about being appointed to the task force. She left out the part about working with Reed because she wasn't going to have that discussion with Javier and she wouldn't be doing anything with Reed but finding a serial killer.

As Javier dropped her off at home she saw her neighbor heading inside with her fiancé. The two looked so wrapped up and in love with each other that Marina felt an acute pang of envy. She wasn't naive enough to think that any successful man would do. A man who stimulated her mentally, physically and emotionally, like Reed Crawford, was what she needed, only better. She started thinking of how she could improve on Reed. After all, he wasn't perfect. After several minutes she gave up, disgusted with herself.

As she settled down at her computer, Marina forced her thoughts back to the task force and Lissa Rawlins. Tomorrow she would find out if Lissa could have killed Elliot Washington and Colton Edwards.

Chapter 4

Marina arrived at the station early the next day to find Reed at his desk, already at work on the computer. "I ran a cross-search of the violent death files on the computer with Merriwhether and hit the jackpot," he said proudly.

"How many did you find?" she asked, praying that several murders hadn't already gone by without someone making a connection.

"Just one. I'm printing the file now."

Stepping around the stack of files on the floor, she stowed her purse in the desk drawer and locked it. Then she dropped into her chair and scooted close to Reed.

The printer whined just behind them and began spitting out the pages. Swiveling her chair around, Marina grabbed the first couple of sheets and began to scan them.

The victim's name was Aubrey Russell. Twenty-seven years old, his body was found behind a popular nightclub, the Hot Spot, in the early morning hours. He'd been stabbed, his body mutilated. He'd also been killed about four months prior to the discovery of Colton Edwards' body. *Four months!* "I think we've got a big lead on the cooling off period between the murders," Marina said, grabbing a pen and a slip of paper to jot down the record number for the file.

Reed's voice sounded close to her ear. "I've already ordered the full file. It has a lot more in it than they put on the computer system."

Marina turned, her face almost colliding with his. She was excited about the new information and knew he was, too, but as their gazes held, something deep inside her heated and she momentarily lost her train of thought. Recovering quickly, she asked, "Did you notice that there was about four months between each of the murders?"

"Yeah, I've sketched out a timeline." He showed her a piece of graph paper where he'd written down the months and marked the date of each murder with a star.

Marina glanced at her watch. It was only a quarter to eight. She worked to keep the note of censure out of her voice. "You've been at this awhile."

"Yeah. I really want to catch this killer and I've got a lot riding on it." Reed rubbed his eyes absently with the sides of his forefingers. "I woke up early this morning thinking about it and decided that I might as well get in here early. We're going to find this killer, whoever he is."

"Yes, we are." Marina inserted her laptop into the docking station. She liked to be first in everything and on a team she drove herself to do her share or more. Right now it looked as if she would have to start getting into the office a little earlier if she wanted to keep up with Reed. "How long before we get the hard copy of the rest of the file?"

Reed stood, tall and broad-shouldered in a deep blue shirt and navy slacks. "It should be ready. I'll go get it right away."

Marina's gaze strayed and she noticed the way the slacks covered his nicely shaped butt and hinted at muscular thighs. Reed had always been something of a contender in the eye-candy department. He had nice, big shoulders and an easygoing walk that radiated confidence. Gritting her teeth, she headed to the coffee area with a big cup. Did he have to look so good this early in the morning?

Together, Marina and Reed studied the details in Aubrey Russell's file. She'd braced herself for what she'd see in the pictures, but her stomach still bucked and her throat froze. Somehow she managed to maintain her dignity. Russell had been stabbed in the chest and abdomen, like the others. He'd also been unmanned, the severed organ left close to the body.

Giving Reed the pictures, she pulled out another section of the file to study. "We need to get down to MUC to get their records," she told him.

He nodded. "I've been thinking the same thing and

I put in for a warrant, but we still don't know what we're looking for. Maybe we should talk to Washington's friends and family first, and see what's been dug up in the investigation? We need more to go on."

Marina glanced at her spreadsheet and agreed that they still knew too little about the victims and the things they had in common. "Has Forensics got enough to give us some preliminary findings?"

Reed checked his watch. "SaintCloud, the forensic specialist assigned to us, said we could come by after nine and he'd be ready."

Reed led Marina through the glass doors of the Forensic Sciences department. Eric SaintCloud was a wiry, intense man of about thirty-five with dark hair and piercing gray eyes. His gaze was steady as he shook Marina's hand firmly. He directed them into his lab area where he'd set up most of the work he'd done so far.

Going through his analysis of the victim's wounds, he informed them that the serial killer had used a knife similar to a common steak knife with a serrated edge on all three victims.

"I found something interesting. None of the three victims had defensive wounds on the hands, arms or forearms of their bodies," Eric said. "Most stab victims have defensive wounds. Preliminary results of blood samples taken from Mr. Washington have been inconclusive, but I suspect that he was drugged. Maybe the others were, too.

"The killer probably used ketamine, a date rape drug, which would have impaired motor function, distorted perceptions of sight and sound, and given him a dream-like feeling. Washington had been drinking, but he wasn't drunk. Samples from the glasses at the scene are being analyzed. Alcohol alone would have slowed his reflexes enough for someone to take him by surprise, but I'm betting that an additional drug immobilized him enough for his attacker to repeatedly stab him."

"How many times?" Marina asked, determined to keep her cool.

"Preliminary count, twenty." SaintCloud didn't skip a beat.

Marina blinked, swallowing a curse. There was a lot of anger and rage in twenty stab wounds. She added the information to the profile she'd been building in her head. "What about the other two victims?"

"Twenty to twenty-five times." SaintCloud turned to remove something from the table. "This was found on Mr. Washington's body." He showed them a magnified photo of a blond hair. "It's from a wig that can be bought in any number of stores in the Chicago area."

"But that doesn't mean that our killer has to be a woman," Marina put in.

"That's true." SaintCloud continued, "Some of the stab wounds were to the chest, but most were below the waist on all three victims. Analysis shows that the attacker stood at least five foot eleven."

Marina nodded. "We need forensics to see if the same knife was used on all the victims, and if the angles and depth of the blows indicate whether we're looking for a man or a woman."

"Already working it," SaintCloud said smugly.

Reed's head came up. "You don't think we're looking for a man? Aren't most serial killers lower- to middle-class white males?"

"Been doing your homework?" Marina teased, raising an eyebrow.

When Reed merely flashed her a lopsided grin in response, she continued. "Yes, most serial killers are male, but the things that have been done to the bodies could also have been done by a woman who hated men."

"It's just less likely," Reed put in.

Marina agreed. "Maybe these guys knew each other. Maybe they knew their killer, too. Then you probably know that serial killers usually choose victims that are vulnerable. I don't see anything in the files that shows these guys as being vulnerable in any way."

Marina left the forensics department with Reed, certain that the evidence supported their initial assumption that all three victims had the same killer. There still wasn't enough information to determine if the killer was male or female.

By nine Reed and Marina had their notebooks and files and were getting into Reed's unmarked car, headed for Lissa Rawlins' place. They didn't call first because Reed didn't want to spook Lissa and give her a chance to run.

Apparently remembering their visit yesterday, the guard in the lobby simply nodded when he saw them.

They buzzed the condo and a woman's sleepy voice answered. Reed gave her their names and asked to be let into the condo. As Lissa buzzed them in, Marina glanced at him in surprise. Taking the small success in stride, Reed pretended not to notice.

Lissa Rawlins opened the door to her loft condo and Reed's first look was enough to make him pause. Lissa was barely dressed in a revealing pair of red baby-doll pajamas and matching red-mink mules. Her double-D-size breasts thrust out like ripe melons. With effort, he focused on her face, made up Marilyn Monroe style. "We can wait for you to put something on," he suggested carefully.

"I'm fine, Lieutenant Crawford," she said, flashing him a smile right off the ad for 1-800-HotBabe. "Come on in and get comfortable."

Reed strode into the high-ceilinged entryway, and onto a patch of the morning sunlight spilling in from the palladium windows. Marina followed close on his heels.

"This is my associate, Special Agent Marina Santos," he added.

Barely nodding at Marina, Lissa faced Reed.

"This is about Elliot, isn't it?"

Marina spoke from just behind Lissa. "Yes, it is."

Lissa ignored her. "Have a seat on the couch," Lissa told Reed. She moved ahead of him, spicing up the view with a provocative rotation of her slim hips.

Glancing back, he almost laughed at the annoyed expression on Marina's pretty face. She hated to be ignored. Was she a little bit jealous, too? He suppressed a smile at the thought. Why should she be comfortable when just being around her kept him on edge? He hadn't gotten over her yet, but he wasn't going to let that or a nearly naked woman stop him from doing his job and finding the serial killer.

Reed took one side of the plush white sofa and Lissa sat with a knee beneath her, effectively taking the rest of the couch with a long leg spanning the distance between them. Marina settled for the matching chair across from them.

"I've been out of town," Lissa explained, "but I knew that sooner or later someone was going to come around asking questions about Elliot. Am I a suspect?"

"I wouldn't go that far," Reed said carefully. "I'd describe you as a person of interest in the case."

Lissa seemed to like that response. She leaned toward him.

He fed her his first question. "When was the last time you saw Elliot?"

Lissa rolled her eyes. "It's been at least a couple of months."

"Where did you see him?" Marina interjected.

Lissa made eye contact with Reed. "I met him at the Hartford Hotel. He was good and it was his favorite place to screw, you know. He paid the staff and they gave him his privacy. I just got tired of being second and third on his list of women. That man was doing me, little Miss Dansinger and whoever else he could get. He couldn't keep it in his pants."

Reed made notes in his little black notebook. "Do you know the names of any of the other women?"

Lissa shrugged. "Except for Jade, I didn't care."

"Some of his friends thought you were stalking him," Marina said.

"And they're lying asses," Lissa countered shrilly. "Elliot asked me to meet him."

Reed studied her, trying to look past her innocent expression to see if she had the will to kill Elliot. He knew she was lying. He held up a file. "I have a copy of a police report he filed, accusing you of stalking him."

"That was before he realized that Jade wasn't nearly enough woman for him," Lissa snapped. "He came to me and begged for it, begged me to come back. It was the best sex we ever had."

"Where have you been the past few days?" Reed asked.

"I was in Detroit, checking on my mother. I wasn't even in town when he got killed and I can prove it. I've got the ticket stubs."

Marina's voice was cool and professional. "We'll need to see those and we'll also need your mother's name, address and phone number so we can check your alibi."

Lissa's eyes widened momentarily, as if she was a little intimidated. "I'll get it for you," she promised Reed.

He went to the next question on his list. "Did you ever see Elliott with a man named Colton Edwards? Or Aubrey Russell?"

Lissa shrugged again. "I don't know. They could have been the guys in that stupid fraternity Elliott used to belong to."

Reed's glance shot up from his notebook. He sensed that this was the break he and Marina had been looking for. "What was the name of his fraternity?"

Sucking her bottom lip, Lissa tilted her head. "Alpha Kappa Epsilon? I think that was it."

Reed's pen sped up. "Did you ever meet any of Elliot's frat brothers?"

Pulling her knees up to her chest, Lissa put her back on the armrest. "No. He didn't want to share me with them. Isn't that a laugh?"

Before Reed could answer they heard the sound of a key turning in the lock. Lissa seemed to grow smaller as she lowered her legs to the floor to sit primly on the other end of the couch.

The atmosphere in the room changed drastically. The man who opened the door was built like a wrestler with a short, powerful body and pugnacious face topped with glossy black curls. "Lissa," he said, taking in her scantily clad form, "why you sitting around guests in your underwear? What are trying to do, huh? Give the man a heart attack?"

"Relax, Tony," she snapped. "They're cops. They came to ask questions about Elliot."

Tony slammed the door shut with an air of barely controlled anger. His wary gazed flicked over Reed and Marina, lingering longer over Marina's breasts and finally her face. "You two got a warrant?"

"No." Marina's tone implied that it wasn't a problem.

Tony gave off powerful waves of suppressed violence as he flicked a thumb at the door. "No warrant, then get out."

Sizing the other man up, Reed spoke. "Tony, chill. We need to see Lissa's airline ticket stubs and proof that she was in Detroit when Elliot Washington was killed or we'll be taking her downtown with us." He didn't know how much control Tony had over himself, but he wasn't taking any chances. His hand was close to the gun he wore strapped at his waist, just beneath his suit jacket.

Lissa scrambled to her feet. "I'll get those stubs for you," she said, hurrying into the back.

Tony approached Reed, his eyes sparking with aggravation. "I don't know why you come here bothering Lissa about that bum. She was over him a long time ago."

Marina stood. "How long have you been with Lissa?"

Tony rotated his shoulders. "About a month or so, why?"

"We need to know where you were the night before last, the night someone killed Elliot Washington. Maybe you decided to take him out of the picture."

"No. I didn't have to kill the bum. I already told you. She was over him," Tony replied angrily, narrowing his eyes.

Marina didn't argue. She simply waited for the answer to her question with an unwavering expression.

"I was playing poker with the boys from about eight

till about two-thirty in the morning. I drank until I passed out."

"You got someone who can verify that?" Reed asked.

"Yeah, Vince Vanetti." Tony rattled off a phone number.

Bent on verifying the alibi, Reed whipped out his cell phone and called the number. Identifying himself as a police officer, he asked about Tony and the card game, deliberately giving the wrong day. Vince, the man on the other end hesitated for moment, and corrected him. Tony had been at his house playing cards, passed out and ended up spending the night. Vince promised to come down to the station to sign a statement.

Reed switched off the phone. Lissa had thrown on a robe and was waiting while Marina copied the numbers and information off her airline ticket stubs. Afterward, Lissa gave Marina a slip of paper with her mother's name and address printed on it.

"You got everything you need from us?" Tony asked, looking as if he'd sat on the sharp edge of a tack.

Reed closed his notebook. "Yeah, but we'll be back if this stuff doesn't check out."

"It will," Tony stormed. "Now get the hell out of our house."

Reed stopped in the act of gathering his things to confront Tony. "Hey, you need to watch your language. We're just doing our jobs and we've treated you with respect. We expect the same back. If it's too hard for you to be civil enough for us to do our jobs here, we can all go down to the station. Understand?"

Tony turned red and his dark brows pulled together like thunderclouds, but his head dipped slightly in acknowledgment.

Reed and Marina made a dignified exit.

"Do you think Lissa did it?" Reed asked as they got into the car.

Marina cinched her seat belt. "No, but before Tony showed up, I was sure she was going to try to get in your underwear. I'm still checking out her alibi. She could have taken a quick flight back here, killed Elliot and gone back to Detroit. If her mother is elderly or sick, how would she know?"

Reed thought back to Lissa's obvious anger with Elliot. Had it been enough for her to kill? And could she have killed Colton Edwards? He'd seen no signs of recognition in her facial expression. They were looking for a serial killer, but they had to make sure that none of the killer's supposed victims had died by another hand.

"For a moment there, I thought you were going to pull a gun on Tony," Marina said as they pulled away from the curb.

Reed kept his eyes on the road as he answered. "For a moment there, I thought I was going to have to."

Marina stretched and yawned in the seat next to him. "It got pretty tense."

"And you loved it," he shot back, enjoying the banter between them and her presence beside him. "If I'd had to draw my gun, you'd have been right there with me." He glanced away from the road to catch a glimpse of her soft berry-coated lips turning upward in response. Heat went through him like lightning. He'd always been a sucker for that smile. He jerked his gaze back to the road.

He guessed that Marina hadn't noticed. Her voice was slow and thoughtful. "Let's pick up the warrant, get something to eat, then head up to Merriwhether. Maybe we can find that frat house."

Tapping the steering wheel, he said, "We need to check university and fraternity records for each of the victims. I'd bet money on the frat being the link between them."

"They're already linked by the fact that they all went to Merriwhether and are pretty close to the same age," she reminded him. She pulled her wallet from the pocket of her jacket. "How much do you want to bet?"

Reed laughed out loud. "I change my mind. I'll bet, but let's not use money. The loser, and that will be *you,* has to do something for the winner."

"What do you want, Reed?" she asked, trademark toughness creeping into her tone. "I wouldn't jump into bed with you if you won the bet."

Inside Reed froze. She had to go there, didn't she? He kept his physical reaction to a minimum. "What makes you think that's what I'd want?" he quipped. He heard her barely audible gasp. It salved the part of him that was still hurting over the way she'd just dropped him for another man.

"Then what do you want?" she asked, trying to read him.

"I don't know," he answered truthfully, "but if you

don't want to do it, I'll settle for this statement, 'Reed you're simply the best, even better than me and I simply don't have the guts to do what you want.'"

Those were fighting words. Out of the corner of his eye he saw her lips tighten. Marina didn't like conceding defeat to anyone.

"Too much for you?" he asked, needling her just a little.

"No. It's a bet," she insisted. "I've just got to think of something embarrassing that I'd like you to do when you lose. And you will lose."

Reed started laughing all over again.

Turning her head, Marina pretended to look out the window.

For lunch, they stopped at a little Greek restaurant close to the Merriwhether University campus to eat. The Greek music playing in the background and the easy atmosphere took Reed back to earlier times when they'd hung out in places like this.

Marina sat next to him in the booth, looking comfortable. Reed didn't buy into the illusion because he felt the weight of her gaze on him whenever she thought he wasn't looking. He'd managed to get her attention this time. Maybe she'd finally realized that she'd made a big mistake. He didn't ever plan to pursue her again, but pride drove him to prove that she'd welcome him if he tried.

"I've got it," Marina said, flashing him a devilish smile. "How about you doing my laundry for a week if you lose the bet?"

Reed's mind conjured up several filmy, silky, lacy

pieces of sexy lingerie that could reasonably be included in Marina's laundry. He swallowed hard.

"Gotcha!" Marina burst into laughter.

"Actually, I'd consider you doing my laundry for a week if you lose," he said, taking some of the sting out of her laughter.

Shaking her head, she finished the last of her salad. "Let's get going," she said, gathering her things. "We've got a serial killer who's probably out there getting ready for the next victim."

Chapter 5

Marina fell silent when they entered the Merriwhether campus and drove past the Paley and Clifford dormitories, the Language, Arts and Sciences building and the Business School. Memories of her graduation, the glory days as a student, her friends, hopes, loves and aspirations echoed back. Coming back always had that effect on her because she had a love for this place and who and what she was then that would forever be a part of her.

"Takes you back a little, huh?"

Acknowledging Reed's question with a nod, she glanced at him, seeing the tall, gangly youth in T-shirt and jeans that he'd been when she'd met him at registration on her first day at Merriwhether. Back then, his beautiful eyes had been hidden behind thick, Clark-

Kent-type glasses and his face had been thin and boyish-looking. She'd been frustrated with the registration process and her inability to get the classes she'd wanted. Reed had shown her how to get on the list for the second section of the class or how to meet the degree requirements with other courses.

Reed parked the car outside the student services building. Inside, they stood with several baby-faced students in the records office line. Flashing their badges and the warrant, they waited while the clerk pulled records and transcripts for Elliot Washington, Colton Edwards and Aubrey Russell. Afterward, they sat on one of the couches in the bustling lobby, studying the records.

Colton Edwards and Elliot Washington had shared a couple of classes with Aubrey Russell. All had also been members of a campus fraternity, Alpha Kappa Epsilon.

Marina glanced at her watch. It was already two o'clock. "Things are looking better for my end of the bet," she said, trying to keep the amusement out of her voice. "Why don't we head over to the frat house before we leave the campus and see what we can get on Edwards, Russell and Washington?"

"We still have a possible class connection, but hold up a minute." Reed walked over to the information desk, which was covered with stacks of pamphlets. Searching through the piles, he triumphantly held up a list of campus frat houses.

Together they studied the pamphlet until they found

Alpha Kappa Epsilon. The address was only six blocks away. They hurried to the car.

The Alpha Kappa Epsilon house was a large white building in the Greco tradition, resembling an old southern mansion. After parking on the street, Reed and Marina mounted the steps and rang the bell.

A fresh-faced blond youth in jeans and a Merri-whether T-shirt answered the door and ushered them inside. Reed asked to speak to someone in charge.

"Are you from the university administration?" the kid asked, looking worried.

"No, I'm from the C.P.D.," Reed said, showing his badge. "And Ms. Santos is from the FBI."

On cue, Marina held up her badge.

The youth's mouth fell open. "Are we in trouble?"

"Well now, that depends," Reed answered, cocking his head to the side.

"I'll get our chapter president." The youth's voice squeaked. He shot out of the room.

Minutes later he returned with a more mature-looking, dark-haired young man.

"Hello. I'm Austin Perry, president of this chapter of Alpha Kappa Epsilon. Ed says you're from the C.P.D. and the FBI?"

"That's correct." Reed moved forward and offered his hand. "Reed Crawford, Chicago P.D."

Marina followed suit. "Marina Santos, FBI."

"What do you want with us?" Austin asked in a voice that shook.

Reed spoke calmly. "We're trying to find a killer who's already eliminated three former members of your fraternity. We need all the information you have on the victims and information on any other members who may fit the same profile."

Austin's eyes rounded. "Who were the victims?"

"Colton Edwards, Aubrey Russell and Elliot Washington."

Myriad expressions crossed Austin's face. One was recognition of the three names. Another was fear associated with that recognition. He suppressed those expressions quickly. "I'm not absolutely certain those three were members. I can't give you any private information, either, without at least a release from our parent organization. And if they were indeed members of this fraternity, I may even need a signed release from their families."

"All the men were definitely members of your fraternity," Marina put in. "We've already gotten their records from the university."

"We—we'll still have to get back to you," Austin insisted.

"Don't take too long," Reed warned him. "We wouldn't want to see another one of your members die, would we?"

Austin backed up. "Are you threatening us?"

Marina took a step forward. "Here's the threat. If we don't get the information we've asked for within a day or two, we'll come back with a search warrant. If any additional members of your fraternity die in the meantime, oh, well…"

"I'm going to call our parent organization and the lawyers right away," Austin assured them. "You should hear from us in a couple days."

"I wonder what they're hiding," Reed remarked as he and Marina left the frat house and made it down the stairs to the car. "It's obvious that they already knew those guys were members."

"Maybe they know why those three were targeted," Marina suggested.

"No, maybe they've got a good idea who the serial killer is," Reed said.

While Marina considered it, he started humming the theme song from the "Twilight Zone" television show.

Marina massaged her forehead with her fingers. This case had been on her mind for the last twenty-four hours straight and she was starting to lose her edge. "And what could a group of college students do that is so reprehensible that they'd rather be hunted by a serial killer than go to the police?"

Reed raised his brows and settled for a wide-eyed stare. "Hmmm I don't know…murder?"

"Murder?" She straightened in her seat, thoughts of the ugly side of human nature increasing the pressure in her head. "Right now anything is possible. All we've got is that they shared some university classes and belonged to Alpha Kappa Epsilon fraternity." She clenched and unclenched her fingers and let her breath out in a huff. "I've just got to take my mind off this case long enough to go to my nephew's birthday party tonight."

"Chico?" Reed asked, turning the car into the station lot and parking.

"Yes, it's Chico's birthday," she replied with a smile, touched that he remembered. "I've got to run." Gathering her things she got out of the car in a rush.

"Enjoy the birthday party," Reed called out as she hurried to her car.

Austin Perry's obvious recognition and fear upon hearing the names Colton Edwards, Aubrey Russell and Elliot Washington's names had haunted Marina all the way back to the station. She decided she would start her research on the victims' names as soon as she got the chance.

Marina went home to freshen up. She donned a hot-pink tank dress and matching sandals. Then she gathered her thick hair into an upsweep and added gold loops to her ears. With a big, gaily wrapped package in tow, she headed to her cousin Carmen's.

Her entire family filled Carmen's little house in Humbolt Park with conversation, music, laughter and singing. It was little Chico's third birthday and his brown button eyes sparkled with the joy of being the absolute center of attention.

Marina liked to pretend that little Chico was her baby. Some day she'd have a precious baby just like him. Lifting the little darling in her arms she swung him around and around until they both were dizzy. Placing him back on his little chair of honor she kissed him and presented him with her gift. The big goofy-looking bear was a huge hit. He covered her cheek with baby kisses, his little arms locking around her neck.

As Marina joined the crowd of well-wishers she found Javier looking suave and debonair at the punch bowl. "No drink and no date, Dad?"

"I told you, I'm turning over a new leaf. What's your excuse?"

She eyed him quizzically. "Do I need one? I just wanted to spend some time with my family."

He gave her an affectionate hug. "That's as good a reason as any. How's the task force coming?"

"It's coming." She kissed his cheek.

"So you're keeping the men of Chicago safe from this serial killer?"

"We're still going through the investigation, Dad. We don't have a suspect yet."

"So we're all in danger then."

"Not everyone, Dad. There's a lot of people who don't fit the profile and we're still working that."

Javier smiled at her. "I just can't get over the fact that my Marina is a hotshot FBI agent."

Marina returned the smile. "I'm proud of you, too, Dad."

"And what did I do?"

"You finished that painting for the recreational center. You've got your own place for the first time in years and you're doing great."

Javier shrugged. "Hey, this being alone is like what they say for Alcoholics Anonymous, one day at a time."

"You *don't* have to do it for me," she reminded him. "I'm claiming my own mistakes these days."

"This break has been good for me, too," he admitted. "I've started thinking about what I really want and why."

"I'm proud of you," she repeated. Minutes later she saw him out in the center of the room doing a salsa with her aunt Anita.

A movement across the room captured her attention. Her cousin Janisa was beckoning to her. She made her way there. The two cousins hugged and sat to catch up on the things that had been going on in their lives. Then Janisa told Marina that she was ready to arrange a blind date between Marina and a friend of her husband's.

Marina opened and closed her mouth in silence. Just the other day she'd been feeling lonely. She couldn't fathom why she wasn't really interested in meeting someone now, even someone prescreened by her family. The thought of learning someone new while she did task force business had no appeal. She decided to pass. "I'm too busy right now," she explained. "Maybe when we've caught this killer and everything has returned to normal."

That was what she told her cousin, but thinking back on how she'd been feeling lately, Marina realized that she hadn't felt lonely since she'd started working the task force with Reed.

Eyeing her speculatively, Janisa nodded and said, "Just let me know when you're ready."

"*Sí.*" Marina hugged her cousin once more. "I will."

Minutes later everyone gathered around the lighted cake to sing "Happy Birthday" to Chico. After a bit of cake and ice cream, Marina said her good nights.

The look she'd seen on the fraternity club president's face still haunted Marina as she made her way home from the family birthday party. She was sure he'd already known the connection between the serial killer's victims and it had been something so bad that the national organization had to get involved in the release of information. What could be that bad? she wondered as she used her key to enter her refurbished brownstone.

The colorful, plush interior was just as warm and inviting as when she'd left it, but she knew all too well what was really missing; someone who loved her. Marina satisfied herself with taking a seat at her contemporary desk and switching on the computer. She played a lot on the Internet, so this did not feel like work.

She started the first search by entering the fraternity's name into the search engine, just to get a general idea. The sight of no less than four hundred fifty thousand results made her sigh. Until she had more of an idea of what she was looking for, it wouldn't do to narrow the search. She waded into the pile, cutting time by reading the short summaries listed on the pages of the search engine.

Halfway down the page she stopped at a result that had her groaning. She'd been in training at the academy when the events in the article had gone down.

> *Several members of the Alpha Kappa Epsilon*
> *fraternity at Chicago's Merriwhether University*
> *have been charged with the rape of a co-ed at the*
> *frat house during Pledge Week. The co-ed, whose*
> *name is being withheld, also accuses frat members*
> *of using a date rape drug. Frat members contend*
> *that the sex was consensual and that a tape was*
> *made of the incident with the co-ed's full knowl-*
> *edge. The university has censored the organiza-*
> *tion. If the charges stick, several members could*
> *go to prison and the fraternity will be banned from*
> *campus. Several campus support groups have*
> *reached out to the victim who has sought and re-*
> *ceived university psychological services.*

Marina skimmed several articles that basically
repeated the facts in the first reference article, which had
been in the *Chicago Tribune*. Then she found another
article that addressed the trial.

> *Things are going badly in court for the prose-*
> *cution team pitting Carrie Ann Gellus against*
> *several members of Merriwhether University's*
> *Alpha Kappa Epsilon fraternity. The fraternity*
> *has benefited greatly from hiring several high-*
> *profile members of the legal community including*
> *Connor Lawrence, Peter Saville and Finnegan*
> *Forbes. A key piece of evidence, the videotape of*
> *the alleged rape, has been rendered all but inef-*

*fective through the skillful efforts of the defense
team. At no point during the taped incident does
Ms. Gellus refuse the advances of the accused.
The prosecution contends that Ms. Gellus had
been drugged and was therefore not fully aware
of what was going on. They have been unable to
prove that a drug was used. Ms. Gellus had ad-
mittedly been drinking and did not remember the
incident until several days later.*

An artist sketch at the end of the article showed Carrie
Ann as a fresh-faced co-ed with blond hair and green
eyes. She looked like an innocent. Marina knew that
people were innocent until proven guilty, but she never
once doubted that Carrie Ann Gellus had been raped.

With an aggravated moan Marina stopped reading to
thrust frustrated fingers through her thick hair. Her head
dipped. She'd known it would be something like this.
Known it. One fist pounded her desk. Sometimes she
hated her job, especially when people harmed others
and hid behind the law, making her the bad guy.

When she felt calmer Marina went back to combing
through the articles. Twenty-year-old Carrie Ann
Gellus had lost the court case. She'd killed herself in
the aftermath.

Beads of sweat broke out on her brow. Marina felt
sick, angry and trapped. The facts made it entirely possible that her serial killer victims were frat house predators who had preyed on female students and got away

with it. It was highly likely that one of their victims or someone close to one of their victims was making sure they now paid for what they'd done.

Marina scanned several articles about the trial for the names of the young men involved. She formed a list: Aubrey Russell, Colton Edwards, John Stuart and Dean Hafner.

Elliot Washington's name was not on the list of young men accused of raping Carrie Ann. Marina pondered that fact. There had to be a connection.

In a few other articles concerning date rape and Merriwhether University, Marina saw that a number of female students had come forward after Carrie Ann's death to report several incidents of date rape and suspected date rape centering on the Alpha Kappa Epsilon fraternity and some other organizations. As a result, the fraternity had been censored and banned from campus for several years.

Marina's thoughts pushed forward as she processed what she'd learned. She couldn't bring herself to read any more of the articles identified by the search engine. There'd be plenty more time for that tomorrow.

It was hard to believe that the answer to her serial killer puzzle would be as simple as scrubbing the list of frat house victims and those close to them, and establishing alibis. That was her next course of action unless Reed had a better idea. Of course she'd also compare her new list of suspects with an FBI profile of the serial killer.

Briefly she toyed with the idea of calling Reed to tell him what she'd discovered, but why ruin what was left of his evening? As she prepared for bed, her mind was still so busy with what she'd discovered that she picked up the phone and called Reed anyway.

He answered in a low, intimate voice that made her want to reach through the phone to touch him. She wondered if he was alone then squashed the thought.

"It's Marina," she explained quickly. "I didn't want to disturb you, but after our trip to Merriwhether today, I did some searching on the Internet and what I found is troubling."

"To say the least," Reed put in quickly. "I've been helping Ma with an Internet dating service, so I did some online searching after that for myself."

"Hey, we're the Merriwhether crew. Great minds think alike," she murmured, trying to imagine Trudy on a date with a guy she'd met on the Internet. Maybe it was something she should steer her dad into. *Not!*

"Did you see the names of the guys involved in the court case with Carrie Ann Gellus?" Reed asked.

Nodding, Marina stretched out across her bed. "Yeah. I copied the list and it includes all our victims so far except for Elliot. There were a couple of new guys, too."

"Think they're in danger?"

Marina adjusted the phone on her ear. "They should at least be warned. We may have to protect them. Then we need to verify this connection between the serial killer victims as soon as possible."

Reed cleared his throat. "If our serial killer maintains

the schedule he's been keeping, we've still got some time to figure this thing out completely."

"Let's not count on that," Marina said, nibbling on her bottom lip. "I'm going to put everything we've got into the database. It'll help us find our killer."

"Why don't we discuss what's really bothering you?" Reed said, hitting her with an arrow seemingly out of the blue.

She swallowed slowly, her free hand massaging her forehead. Reed knew her all too well. Keeping the edge out of her voice was a struggle. "I think these guys are lowlifes and scum, Reed. I think they raped a lot of women on campus using the date rape drug, alcohol and brute force, and they got away with it."

"Did you finish reading all the articles in the search engine?"

"No." She wasn't about to tell him that tonight she'd lacked the stomach for it. She'd find it tomorrow, get all the facts, and do a damned good job. Tonight she had the luxury of easing her conscience and getting mentally prepared for what was sure to come.

"You don't have all the information so don't be so quick to judge. It's not our job anyway, remember? We're trying to catch a serial killer."

"I don't need you to remind me of my job," she snapped. She softened her tone. "My job is to protect the innocent."

"Those guys from Alpha Kappa Epsilon won the court case, Marina. That makes them innocent."

Marina spoke from her heart. "In the eyes of the law, yes, but you can't tell me that we don't all answer to a Higher Authority."

"No, I won't, because I believe in God. If those guys really did rape Carrie Ann Gellus, they'll have to answer for it. Don't beat yourself up over this, Marina. We'll do our jobs the best we can, whether we like it or not."

"Like it or not," she repeated halfheartedly.

"Are you going to be okay?" Reed's voice oozed compassion and understanding. "Do you want me to come over there?"

Marina sighed. Of course she would be okay. She'd simply needed to talk. The eagerness that leaped through her at his offer to come over was downright embarrassing. It made her want to slap herself. Was she that eager to see Reed at eleven o'clock at night?

"Marina?" The concern and caring in his voice was like a mental caress.

"I—I'm fine," she managed to say. "I just needed to talk."

"So I'll see you in the morning?"

"Yeah," she answered. "Have a good night."

With his salutation Marina pried the phone from her ear and placed it back on the cradle. Covering her eyes with her fingers she moaned, "What is wrong with me?"

Later, as she climbed between the sheets, the answer was all too obvious. She was falling for Reed Crawford again.

Chapter 6

Marina arrived early the next day to finish going through the search engine results. Reed had been right in his assertion that she'd been jumping to conclusions. Although the guys from Alpha Kappa Epsilon accused of rape had been found not guilty, a separate case against two other members had been successful and several female students had come forward to complain to the college administration and the police about the treatment of women at the Alpha Kappa Epsilon fraternity house. The fraternity was banned from campus for several years and two members had actually gone to jail for raping a female student, Jody Payton.

Marina added the names of the convicted rapists, Roger Thayer and Darrel Purvis to her list of likely serial killer targets. She added a note to check to see if they were still in prison. Based on the articles she'd read, they were. Then she added Jody's name and Carrie Ann's sister, Sherianne, to the list of people she and Reed needed to talk to.

Reed arrived around a quarter to eight laden with Starbucks' coffee and a small bag of pastries and bagels. "You okay? I figured you'd get in early," he explained, unloading the feast on the edges of both their desks.

"I'm fine," she assured him, then thanked him for bringing breakfast. "Let me show you what I've come up with."

Reed read through the list that included Lissa, Elliot's ex-girlfriend, Jody Payton, the woman who had been raped and taken the group to court, and Sherianne Gellus, Carrie Ann's sister. "Any male suspects? How about someone refused entry into the fraternity?"

Marina inclined her head. "I can't imagine us finding that in any records. We'll have to ask some of the guys."

"There's only women on this list," he remarked between sips of coffee. "I know I'm repeating myself, but isn't the average serial killer a lower- to middle-class white male in his twenties or thirties?"

Marina licked the cream cheese off her lips. "Yeah, but maybe we're not really looking for a serial killer. Maybe we're looking for a serial avenger."

Reed's eyes darkened. Swallowing, he speared her with a glance. "Serial avenger as in someone avenging wrongdoing like a rape on a college campus?"

Marina shrugged. "Why not? It's the strongest thing we have to go on. And remember, there have been female serial killers."

Reed stated rummaging in a pile of folders on his desk that had come out of his briefcase. Checking the label on one, he handed it over. "I don't think you've seen this."

Marina checked the C.P.D. label. "'Serial Killer Profile for Washington, Russell and Edwards Murders.' No, I haven't seen this. When did it come in?"

Reed's gaze was steady. "Yesterday. I saw it just before we took off for Merriwhether. I didn't get a chance to look at it, so I took it home. I wasn't holding out on you, Marina, I just forgot about it for a little bit."

She let her lips curve upward. "I don't think you were trying to hold out on me," she admitted, "but maybe you should start doing something about the early onset of Alzheimer's."

"Funny, real funny." Visibly relaxing, Reed sat back in his chair.

Marina opened the file. "What do you think?"

Reed tapped his fingers on the desk. "Just read it. I'm not sure it'll be that useful."

She scanned the paragraphs.

Killer is most likely a white male in his mid-twenties to early thirties who knew each victim through an association with Merriwhether University. Killer appears quiet and unassuming but

> *harbors rage against the victims due to their per-*
> *ceived prowess and success with women. Killer*
> *may also harbor resentment from slights or imag-*
> *ined slights that occurred during his time at Mer-*
> *riwhether. This could also include someone*
> *refused entry into the fraternity.*

Marina tossed the file onto her desk. "Perceived prowess and success with women my ass!"

Reed chuckled. "It'll probably get adjusted when we tell them what we found at Merriwhether and on the Internet."

"I hate to see stuff like this in conjunction with Merriwhether. It's like a slur on the name of our school," she admitted.

"You wouldn't want them to cover this up, would you?"

Fisting her ink pen, Marina tapped her open notebook with it. "Hell, no. But if the university administration had jumped on this when the complaints started, it probably wouldn't have gotten so bad."

"Maybe, maybe not," Reed countered diplomatically. "Let's work the list of potential victims and suspects for addresses and phone numbers."

Marina eyed the program on her laptop. "I'm with you, but I've got to finish the information for VICAP first."

Reed leaned forward on his desk. "And what's that going to buy us again?"

"When I put our case information in VICAP, we should get a list of other crimes that could have been committed by our killer and some behavioral clues to help us find him or her."

"Fine. How much do you have left to do?"

"A couple of hours."

"Well maybe we can check out some of the people on the list after lunch."

Marina tapped her desk. "I'm in."

Between the Merriwhether University records office and the Illinois Department of Motor Vehicles, Reed was able to locate an address and phone number for Sherianne Gellus in Palantine, Illinois.

Making their way through the lunchtime traffic, Reed and Marina arrived at Sherianne Gellus' office building. It was in a strip mall off Colonial Parkway.

The gold-edged sign above the door of the brown brick structure sported the names Cameron, Webster and Leslie in elegant black letters. Sherianne was an associate in the law firm.

One of the secretaries showed Reed and Marina back to Sherianne's small office. Blond and fresh-faced as her sister had been, Sherianne was taller, more solidly built, and there was a hard glint in her green eyes.

As soon as the office door closed, Sherianne's polite smile disappeared. "Can you refresh me on why you're questioning me?"

Reed told her that they were looking into the murders of some young men who had gone to Merriwhether University.

"Which young men?" Sherianne's expression gave nothing away.

Marina answered. "We don't know if there have been other victims yet, but so far we have Elliot Washington, Colton Edwards and Aubrey Russell."

"I'm not sorry about those deaths," Sherianne stated flatly, "but then I think you know why. Those men were rapists. They used the date rape drug on my sister, raped her and then lied about it in court. They hurt other women on campus, too, and got away with it."

"I'm sorry about what happened to your sister, but as you know, the young men accused of raping her were proven innocent in court," Reed said, fixing Sherianne with a sympathetic glance.

The pencil in Sherianne's fingers snapped. She shot Reed a look filled with fire. "Yes, because the local prosecutor's office was nothing against the hot-shot lawyers the fraternity hired. Why do you think I went to law school? I've never forgiven myself for not being able to do more to help my sister. I don't know a single person who really believed they were innocent. They bragged about what they got away with."

"Did you feel that you needed to do something to make them pay for what they had done?" Marina asked softly.

"Yes. Hell, yes, I needed to do something to make them pay. That's why I'm a lawyer, that's why I'm still in counseling and that's why I take rape cases for free."

Sherianne's eyes were shiny with tears.

"So you had nothing to do with the deaths of Colton Edwards, Aubrey Russell and Elliot Washington?"

"No, nothing." Sherianne grabbed a tissue from the box on her desk and blew her nose. "But I'll tell you one thing," she continued in a gritty tone. "When you find your murderer, whoever it is, I'm volunteering for the defense team, free of charge. And I'm a *damned* good lawyer."

In the stunned silence, Reed made notes.

Marina studied hers and realized that they had yet to ask a crucial question. "Ms. Gellus, I can understand your anger and hatred for the men accused of raping your sister, but Elliot Washington wasn't one of them."

"That's because he was Carrie's ex-boyfriend and she willingly had sex with him. He was the reason she was at that frat house in the first place!"

A tear slipped down Sherianne's cheek.

There's no accounting for the depths some people will sink to, Marina thought. With an effort, she closed her mouth. Something tied her insides so tight she had to force air into her lungs. She should be used to situations like this, but she wasn't. Her sympathies were with Sherianne and despite the other woman's edgy personality, she felt like a bully. After all, what would she do if she knew men who hurt her cousins and got away with it? She didn't even want to think about it.

Marina straightened in her chair. "Do you suppose Elliot was the one who gave your sister the date rape drug?"

"Yes, I do." Sherianne grabbed another tissue and wiped at her eyes. "I—I tried to talk to Carrie about it, but she wouldn't even consider it. She had blinders on as far as he was concerned."

Reed read the date that Elliot had been killed and asked Sherianne where she was and what she'd been doing on that night.

Sherianne faced him head-on. "I was with my boyfriend, Wyatt Ames, that evening and all night."

"What were you doing on February eighteenth?" Marina asked. That was the night Colton Edwards had been killed.

"Now that I'll have to look up." Sherianne pulled her open desk calendar closer and flipped through the pages. "I was in New York, meeting with one of our major clients."

Marina cast her a doubtful glance. "All night?"

The other woman actually smiled. "No, but you don't think I grabbed a late flight back to Chicago, killed one of those men, and then flew back to New York, do you?"

Marina didn't answer. If she'd been in Sherianne's shoes she might have done it in a heartbeat.

"We'll need the name of your client and the hotel you used so we can check it out," Reed said.

"I'll have our secretary get you a copy of my travel voucher and I have one of Wyatt's cards," Sherianne said. "Is there anything else?"

"We need your alibi for October fourteenth of last year, too," Marina said.

Sherianne made a show of retrieving her appointment book from a desk drawer and checking the date. There was nothing written on that date. Sherianne closed her appointment book, looking a little less confident. "I'm going to have to get back to you on that one. Maybe Wyatt or one of my friends can help me remember."

Thanking her, Marina accepted one of Wyatt's cards and waited for the secretary to make a copy of Sherianne's travel voucher.

With the information in hand, Reed and Marina prepared to leave. "Thanks for making this process easier," Marina said. "We'll get back to you if we have more questions."

Sherianne eyed them speculatively. "Will you tell me when I'm cleared?"

"You're not exactly a suspect," Reed assured her, "but you'll know if we can't verify your alibi and you become a suspect."

Marina rode back to the station deep in thought. Sometimes there was just no justice for the innocent victims. She sympathized with Sherianne Gellus more than she would ever admit out loud, but knew that if Sherianne proved to be their serial killer, she would bring her in. Her feelings didn't matter when it came down to a killer. As she watched Chicago scenery whiz by, she actually found herself praying that Sherianne Gellus was not the killer.

She felt Reed's gaze on her for long stretches of highway and when they stopped for red lights, but he maintained the silence. She appreciated that. When their glances met, she gave him a smile and went back to looking out the window.

Back at the station Reed wasted no time in calling Wyatt and verifying Sherianne's alibi for the night of Elliot Washington's murder. Wyatt wasn't sure if he'd been with Sherianne on October fourteenth of last year, but he was trying to figure it out. Reed arranged for Wyatt to come in to sign a statement.

Marina busied herself with confirming that her data had been received and entered into the VICAP database. She didn't even look up when Reed left the room.

The fragrant scent of strong coffee preceded Reed as he reentered the room. "Coffee?"

Marina pushed her laptop safely out of the way. "Sure, thanks." She sipped the hot liquid, abruptly aware that she had a low-level headache. She needed another coffee. Reed had fixed hers the way she liked it, with lots of cream and sugar. With a satisfied sigh, she drank deeply.

With his own steaming cup of coffee Reed eased back into the seat next to hers. "Want to talk about Sherianne Gellus? Get it off your chest and out in the open?"

"What was this? A bribe?" she asked, swallowing and removing the cup from her lips.

Reed chuckled. "I've been trained in interrogation tactics so I know how to loosen tongues. Seriously though, she had good reason and enough anger to go after Elliot and Colton."

Marina glanced at him from beneath her lashes. "But what about Aubrey? She had no reason to go after him."

"Maybe it's a case of anyone who was part of the fraternity at the time her sister was assaulted is fair game."

"I don't think so." Marina shook her head. "It's something more. I'd bet money on it."

"Speaking of which, you lost the bet we made yesterday. Remember? I bet you that the link between the victims would be that fraternity."

"The jury's still out on that one," she reminded him. "There could be other victims and we still don't know why they're being killed."

Reed expelled the air in his lungs in a huff. "Huh, we've got a damned good idea. It looks like we've got a serial avenger at work here."

"The operative words are 'looks like,'" she reminded him.

"All right. Anything to keep me from winning the bet," Reed whined, just to be annoying.

"I always pay my debts," she reminded him, "even if it means buttering your ego with that little statement you dreamed up."

"Or doing whatever else it is I want you to do," he added.

Marina tossed him a saccharine smile. "Let's get back to work, Lieutenant."

"Don't tell me I'm getting on your nerves," Reed taunted.

"All right, I won't tell you."

Reed made a harsh sound in the back of his throat. "I've been working hard, so I'm going to enjoy my coffee break. If you don't want to talk, I'll find something else to do."

Realizing that he was serious, she stopped him. "Wait, Reed. I'm sorry. I *would* like to talk to you. I'm just a little edgy 'cause I've got a headache."

He dropped back down into his chair. "Waited too long to drink that coffee, huh?"

"Something like that," she admitted. "So how's Trudy?"

Reed gave her a halfhearted grin. "She's happy. She's got a date scheduled with some guy she met on the Internet dating service. If he tries anything, I'll break his legs. I've been a nervous wreck trying to think of ways to protect her."

"So what did you decide on?" she asked, figuring that he had had to come up with something sneaky to get around Trudy. He wasn't going to tell her, but Marina maintained eye contact and waited him out.

"We're going on a double date," he confessed finally.

Marina laughed out loud. "You, Trudy, her date and who else?"

Reed eyed her speculatively. "I hadn't really decided."

She smiled back, waiting for him to ask her. He wanted to, she could see it in his eyes. She even decided that she would say yes because she knew that a night out with Reed and Trudy would be a lot of fun.

The silence grew long and Marina's smile faded

naturally. She watched Reed finish his coffee and get back to work. Staring down at her list of suspects, she worked on keeping her expression neutral, but deep inside the little exchange with Reed felt like a rejection and it hurt.

Chapter 7

It was Reed's turn to care for his mother and he was running late. He came up the side street and turned onto her street. It was sort of dark because the streetlights were out again. The porch lights on the neighboring homes saved the street from looking truly dangerous, but Reed wasn't fooled. There were still a lot of shadows that the porch lights failed to penetrate.

Coming in at night, whether at his own place or his mother's, had become complicated as he grew more and more convinced he was being stalked. He refused to believe it had anything to do with the task force. At his house last night the menace in the dark had turned out to be a stray cat. Tonight he was looking for a bigger culprit. Someone had been playing a cat-and-mouse game with him and he was determined to find out who and end it once and for all. He only hoped none of it spilled over and caused his mother or anyone else to get hurt.

Switching off the ignition, he pulled out his flashlight, checked his gun and put it away. He didn't really think he was going to have to shoot anyone; he was in the old neighborhood, after all. Things had changed, but he still knew a lot of people here and a few that remained had been his friends.

Reed opened the door of his truck and climbed out into warm summer air. The sound of crickets and the faint sound of cars on the street two blocks over filled the night. He shone the flashlight up and down the street and found only a squirrel, an owl and a cat slipping into one of the yards.

Someone was watching him. He could feel it. The back of his neck itched. Senses tingling like crazy, he left the street and walked up the sidewalk to traverse the area between his mother's home and the neighboring one.

Tensing, he headed into the back with his flashlight illuminating the way. None of the sounds that reached him were anything out of the ordinary, but he felt a lurking presence. Focusing, he looked for an attacker. His imagination was going crazy. What if there was more than one of them? What if they were intent on doing more than roughing him up? What if they wanted to kill him?

Shaking the useless questioning process from his mind, he rounded the back of the house. He could handle this.

Out of nowhere a hand caught his wrist and tugged him forward into a hard fist. *"Oomph!"*

Reed literally saw shards of light piercing the dark as his head jerked back on his neck with the impact. The flashlight went tumbling to the ground. Reacting quickly, he threw solid punches to his attacker's torso. His face and eye hurt like hell.

As he maneuvered back and forth with his opponent, Reed couldn't shake the certainty that he knew his attacker. In the dark, he couldn't see the other man's face beneath the stocking cap. Both men grunted beneath the brutal force of the blows given and taken. A combination of skill and luck kept both men on their feet.

Reed went on the offensive. Maneuvering the other man with his fists and placement of his body, he forced the fight toward the side of the garage.

The bright light in front of the garage came on suddenly, blinding Reed.

"Reed? Reed is that you?" his mother called from an opening in her bedroom window.

He maintained his concentration, throwing a hard right that rocked his opponent's head back. He followed it up with a left and watched his attacker warily through slitted eyes. They were both panting. The other man backed into the shadows near the corner of the garage with just a bit of his face and dark hair readily visible.

With one eye swelling and sweat dripping into the other, Reed was a sorry case. He needed to press his advantage and nab this guy. "Yeah. Gimme a minute," he rasped in an effort to soothe her nerves.

"I'm calling the police," she called back.

Reed pressed forward on a savage surge of adrenaline. He couldn't afford to let her distract him any further.

The other man threw a barrage of butterfly punches. It was a setup.

Blocking and stepping back a bit, Reed sparred and looked for the right moment to throw his best right fist.

In a surprisingly gutless move his attacker turned and ran for the back fence.

"Hey!" Reed called after him. Pursuing, he closed on the back fence just as his attacker gracefully leaped up and over. Reed followed, lifting himself on arms that trembled and cursing himself for not spending more of his workout time running.

Charging after the other man, Reed redeemed himself as he steadily reduced the distance between them. Lungs burning, he ran on, intent on catching his quarry. "Stop! Police!" he shouted.

The other man ducked into another yard just as a police squad car drove up and swerved around, effectively blocking the alley.

Reed's attacker had disappeared. Reed flashed his badge and ID, then the two uniformed patrolmen helped him search the area.

Following Reed back to his mother's house, the officers made a report and then left for another call.

The entire incident made Reed mad enough to bite a

brick. His knuckles were swollen and the sucker punch had left him with a black eye. Next time, if there was a next time, he'd be ready.

Inside the house, his mother tried to fuss over him, offering to defrost a steak for his face and eye or to make him an ice pack. Reed used some of the adrenaline still surging through his veins to fix his own ice pack.

"Honey, I'm so sorry. You've been trying to tell me just how much this neighborhood has changed. I love it here so much I haven't wanted to hear it," she mused sadly as he stuffed ice cubes into the pack.

"It ain't about the neighborhood," he said with certainty. "This is about a coward who won't face me in the daylight. It's *on* anytime I come in my place or yours at night. This is personal."

Trudy Crawford gave him a doubtful glance. "You've still got friends in this neighborhood. Who could have it in for you? What about you busting Chelsie Hawkins for killing his girlfriend? Maybe someone thinks you had something to do with the big drug bust over on Platter Street. Most folks here were glad to have the riffraff removed from the neighborhood."

Bristling, Reed shook his head. "I don't know. It could even have something to do with the task force at work, but I think that's a stretch."

"Whoever it is, I don't like seeing your handsome face messed up like that," she mused.

"Really?" he mocked. "Put yourself in my shoes." He winced as he placed the pack on his face, covering the eye.

"Why didn't you call the police?"

"I am the police!" he exclaimed.

"Well, couldn't you have asked for backup?"

"Against what?" Reed adjusted the icepack on his eye and the swollen part of his face. "People watching in the dark? Someone throwing a bottle? I never really saw anyone or had any contact until tonight."

His mother patted his hand. "You'll still fill out a report on this?"

Reed nodded. He really wouldn't have much of a choice anyway. From what he could see, he had a black eye. The swelling wasn't going down, either.

Insisting that his mother get her rest, Reed left the house. Just outside he spent several moments staring into the dark. The cat-and-mouse game had been getting on his nerves, so he was glad that there'd finally been some real action. Most exasperating was an opponent bold enough to sucker punch you in the dark and spineless enough to run away when real action resulted.

Taking the steps, Reed put more swagger in his walk. He was ready for more action, whenever it came.

The next morning Marina took one look at Reed and stared, momentarily speechless. He had a black eye and one side of his face looked slightly swollen. "You get in a fight?"

"Someone in the old neighborhood caught me in the dark last night and sucker punched me. We fought, but he got away."

"You do a police report?"

He nodded. "They came out and did a preliminary. I finished up this morning."

"So what'd they say?"

"They'll watch the house. I can call for backup whenever I'm in the area."

"Next time you visit Trudy, I want to do backup." Marina huffed. She knew Reed could take care of himself, but the need to pound whoever had sucker punched Reed to a pulp was so strong her hand formed a fist.

"I'm a big boy. I don't need your protection." He virtually snarled.

"Okay." Chalking it up to sore bear syndrome, Marina moved closer to examine his battered face. She wanted to gently smooth the dark hair back from his forehead and to take the pain away. She wanted to give him a hug. Neither would be professional behavior and neither would be appreciated. To get herself past the emotional moment, she blinked a couple of times. Then she realized she was holding her breath.

Reed scowled at her. "You looked your fill?"

As usual, Marina rose to the challenge. "Not exactly. I've never seen you like this. Are you sure it has nothing to do with what we're doing on the task force?"

He shot her an impatient glance. "What's there to consider? I've never been in that damned fraternity."

"Maybe we're getting too close to the killer."

Reed expelled a breath on a huff. "We've got nothing but a list of suspects and a lot of questions."

Marina glowered at him. "My goal for today is to whittle that list down. You can spend the day snarling in your corner or you can help."

"Back down, tiger," Reed admonished. "I had planned to help. I'm part of this team, too, remember?"

Satisfied, Marina nodded. "Coffee?"

"Yeah."

She passed him a cup of the gourmet blend she'd picked up on the way in.

Thanking her, he sipped it gratefully. "Since I was in early, I scanned the list on the student activities chart for Merriwhether and found the Women's Campus Crisis Center and the Student Advocate Office. Between the two, we should be able to get a list of all the victims and the accused."

"What about the warrant for records from Alpha Kappa Epsilon?" Marina asked, combing through the stack of papers on her desk.

"We should have it today, along with the warrant for you to search records at crisis center and student advocate offices. It's on my list to check with Judge Stevens' staff.

Around ten, Reed got his warrant and took off for Merriwhether. Marina rode with him, but she had appointments with the Women's Campus Crisis Center staff and the Student Advocate Office.

At the crisis center, Marina interviewed Nona Richard, a slender, chocolate-skinned, African-American woman with a short afro and big earrings. A former student, she was now one of the staff members. In a calm, no-nonsense style, Nona informed her that under the leadership of one of its worst college presidents, Merriwhether had gone through a shameful period where an unusual number of women on campus had been preyed upon. Many of the resulting accusations of rape and assault had been buried in administrative bureaucracy. Other complaints had died in the police bureaucracy due to lack of evidence.

Of the few cases that made it to court, the most famous was the case of Carrie Ann Gellus, a female student who lost her case due to the skillful maneuverings of the high-profile lawyers representing the Alpha Kappa Epsilon fraternity. Carrie's death signaled hard times for the fraternity and the university when it became clear that the university had not followed federal law mandates for college campus handling of rape and assault victims and their rights.

Sitting across from Marina in a navy-blue summer suit, Nona's eyes sparkled with heartfelt emotion. "Understand, the Gellus case wasn't the only one. There were a few that were successful in terms of convictions and sentencing."

Marina showed Nona the search warrant. Accepting a file from Nona, Marina scanned for the names of the serial killer's victims. They were all there. There were also accused men on the list who were not members of the fraternity and some from the local population who had entered the campus to prey on the female students.

"That's confidential information," Nona reminded Marina.

"Of course. The information will be processed and used by the task force to help find the killer." Marina scanned the pictures decorating the office walls. Several depicted groups of women protesting and conducting strategy meetings. There were also pictures of staff members outside the courthouse, physically and emotionally supporting what Marina guessed were some of the rape victims.

Marina pointed to an emotional scene on the courthouse steps. Friends and supporters held two crying women while a third woman faced the media in front of the courthouse. The picture told an emotional story that pulled at Marina, eliciting more emotion than she was ready to give.

"Was that picture taken during one of the trials?" she asked.

Nona's gaze focused on the picture. She smiled. "Yes. That's Elizabeth Hatcher, the first director of the crisis center, facing the media. She fought the university for funding and a charter to set up the Women's Campus Crisis Center. We didn't have much staff then, so she gave a lot of herself. She really was a catalyst for changing things for women on this campus."

"Where is she now?" Marina asked. She wondered how far Elizabeth had taken her job as catalyst. Had she led the women she helped past the lines of legally acceptable behavior? Something in the emotional scenes pictured on the wall made Marina think that Elizabeth Hatcher would have information pertinent to her case.

"Actually she's gotten her doctorate, and moved on to head up the Victim's Crisis Center over at St. Joseph Hospital. She's still in the news from time to time. We're very proud of her. I have one of her cards if you'd like to get in touch with her."

Marina studied the notes she'd made. "I would. Thanks."

"It must be hard for you," Nona remarked as she made copies of the files for Marina.

Marina glanced up from removing the staples from a stack of sheets. "What's hard?"

"I was just thinking out loud. I meant that it must be hard for you to go after a killer who has been avenging crimes against helpless women."

Marina froze. If she'd been thinking it herself, it was only a matter of time before someone else mentioned it, she reasoned. Lifting her head, she met Nona's gaze without blinking. "Last time I checked, murder was a crime."

"Yes, but you know what I mean. What's happening is a sort of justice in itself."

Marina shook her head. "I can't let that matter. I've sworn to do my job and uphold the law, no matter where my sympathies lie."

Nona's brows went up. "Well you have *my* sympathies." She went back to copying the documents.

Marina stared at her, wishing she could read Nona's

mind. Nona had a hunch or knew something important about the serial killer. "Do you know who might be killing those men?" Marina asked point blank.

Taking the stack of copies from the hopper, Nona's lips settled into a stubborn line. Her eyes were hard. "Of course not."

"Withholding evidence is a crime," Marina reminded her.

"But I'm giving you plenty of evidence." Nona handed Marina two of the stacks of copies.

Marina didn't bother to respond. If she didn't get the information she needed, she'd come back to grill Nona.

Stashing the copies in her briefcase, Marina thanked Nona for her help. Then she left the crisis center and went two buildings down to the Student Advocate Office.

The office was housed in the building that used to be the Student Activities Center, so it was big. The interior had been remodeled to provide separate offices for each of the staff members and a couple of conference rooms.

A boyish-looking redhead in an Oxford shirt and dark slacks, Brennan Stallworth, was the chief of the Student Advocate Office. He studied Marina's badge and ID carefully. Then he pulled out a bunch of folders and rested his folded hands upon them.

"Most women attacked on campus during the period you inquired about were either processed through the Women's Campus Crisis Center, which was a fledgling organization at the time, or they were processed through the local police. Most of the complaints died in the administrative process for a variety of reasons. The women who came to the Student Advocate Office were out of the norm. They were fighters and they were determined to see justice done for the crimes committed against them."

"And did they get justice?" Marina asked, studying him.

Brennan inclined his head. "Some did. Nothing is ever one hundred percent guaranteed.

"How did your office help them?" Marina asked.

"In several cases we interceded with the university to argue for their rights and get them fair treatment. We supported several of the students who took the legal route by lending a hand with evidence gathering. We also helped others through the university process to pursue punitive measures against their attackers."

"Is that all?" Marina fought hard to keep the disappointment out of her voice.

"We also brought several of the victims together and they formed support groups."

Support groups? Marina knew that victims often banded together to form a psychological bond to help one another through a shared traumatic experience. She wondered if this could be the key to her serial killer. "Do you have documentation on the support groups?"

Brennan shrugged. "It really wasn't an official function of this office. It sort of happened and it seemed to help more than anything else as far as moral support to the victims. We had to stop referring people to the support groups when a couple of the members got together and physically attacked a male student on campus."

She stopped writing in her notebook to lean forward. "Was the male student who was attacked one of those accused of rape or assault?"

Brennan nodded. "Yes, but the university could not condone any sort of vigilante justice. It also caused problems for us since our office receives federal funding through the university."

"Do you have the names of the women involved and the male student who was attacked?"

"There's a copy of the campus police record of the incident in one of the files. It should have everything you need."

"May I see them now?" Marina asked, holding out her hands.

"Certainly." Brennan stood. Walking to a desk in a corner of the room, he placed the folders on it. "You can use this desk while you go through the files. We have a copy machine in the back that you can use to copy the documents you need."

Thanking him, Marina settled herself at the desk and started scanning the material in the folders. Her first task was to find the campus police record and get the name of the victim and two women involved in the vigilante incident. She found the information buried in the middle of the stack.

Marina read the campus police record twice. One of the names in it flashed in her brain like a red alert. She was on to something. Containing her excitement, she attached a sticky note to mark the file containing the record and placed it in the pile of items to be copied.

Because of the way the material was organized, it took some effort for Marina to tag the different support groups and their participants. The group with the women who had attacked the male student on campus was a major part of her search. Finally she placed all material with references to the support groups into the pile of material to be copied.

With her briefcase full of copied documents, Marina strolled to the place where she'd agreed to meet Reed.

On the grass beneath a tree with his knees drawn to his chest, Reed was people watching and enjoying the day. He wore the black eye like a badge of courage, but the sight of it still made her angry.

"Did you get the info on the frat boys?" she asked, taking a seat beside him. The simple act resonated with her, bringing back myriad memories of days like this.

"I got it." Reed shifted so she could rest her back against the trunk of the tree. "They were prepared to give us a minimum of information so it was a good thing we had the warrant. They're a slimy group if I say so myself."

"Here, here," Marina agreed. "Details on their slimi- ness?"

"They videotaped what they did to Carrie Ann and were selling it on the Internet. Sherianne found out and took legal action to make them stop. She also used it, among other things, to get them banned from campus."

Marina shuddered. To be violated the way Carrie Ann had been was unforgivable, but to be violated and have it made so public was more than anyone should have to bear. "Before or after she killed herself?"

Reed's head dipped. "Before."

Marina forced her throat to work. Sometimes she hated her job. "Anything else?"

"She wasn't the only victim they taped. Several tapes were confiscated by the police." Reed plucked a blade of grass and carefully shredded it with his fingers. "Their records show that Elliot was one of the ringleaders in the aggressive behavior against women. The fraternity's reputation took a nosedive when he and some of his buddies joined. Since Elliot used to be Carrie Ann's boyfriend, he convinced her that he wasn't involved."

Rubbing her forehead with a forefinger, Marina nodded. "Did you get a list of all the members accused of rape and assault?"

"Yes. It's in the car and all our victims are on it." Reed got to his feet. "We should be getting back."

In the car on the way back to the station Reed asked about her visit to the Women's Campus Crisis Center and the Student Advocate Office.

She told him about the support groups formed with the help of the student advocate and crisis center offices and the vigilante attack on a male student. Then Marina dropped the bomb. "The male student attacked on campus was Aubrey Russell. In addition, one of the women involved in the attack was in a support group with Nona Richard and Sherianne Gellus. She got six months in jail and two years probation."

Reed's gaze met hers briefly. "This has got vigilante justice written all over it," he said in a grim tone. "The question is, why did they stop the attacks on the frat members and why have they started up again?"

Marina turned as much as her seat belt would allow. "I've got a theory on that, too. If we're tagging the right suspects, they may have stopped because one of the women involved in the attack was in jail and then on probation. I'll check, but I'm almost certain her probation ended within the last year."

"So who's the next victim?" Reed asked, accelerating onto the freeway.

Marina hesitated then shook her head. "I don't know, but I was going to try to work that out tonight."

"*We'll* try to work it out tonight," Reed confirmed.

"Fine." Marina stiffened a smile and swallowed a snappy comeback. She hadn't meant to leave Reed out of it. She'd simply been focused on solving the case.

"I'm not sticking around the damned office, either," Reed continued. "Your place or mine?"

"Mine. I'll even spring for dinner," Marina said, thinking she could whip up something quick.

"What time should I show up?"

"Uh, six-thirty or seven." The sudden rush of excitement caused her to lean forward and adjust the air conditioning vents. She reminded herself that this was not a date. Still, this would be the first time Reed would visit her new place.

"Do you want me to bring anything?" Reed's question cut into her quick mental survey of what she could serve for dinner.

"Just yourself and all your case info. I'll have everything else we need."

Back at the station they stopped in the office to get their files. Reed took some time to go brief his captain on their progress. Marina called into her office and updated Spaulding. He was adamant that they arrange protection for the potential frat victims as soon as they were identified.

As Marina drove home she was a bundle of nerves and tension. Inwardly she chastised herself for getting so excited about seeing a guy she'd dumped. The truth was that she'd made a mistake and despite her attempts to move on, something inside her still quickened at the sight of Reed. Could she turn things around? Should she even try?

Through pure force of will Marina turned her thoughts to catching the serial killer. The task force investigation had been going smoothly so far. She liked brainteasers, gathering and analyzing information to find serial killers, but she wasn't dumb enough to think that the killer would sit on his or her hands in the meantime. In the back of her thoughts was the fear that through action or inaction she might not be able to save the next victim. It sobered her and counterbalanced her hormonal reaction to Reed Crawford. If it killed her, she and Reed would make real progress on the case tonight.

Chapter 8

Marina rushed home in a quandary about what she could cook fast that would be enjoyed by both her and Reed. She had all the ingredients for *asopao de pollo*—chicken soup—in the refrigerator, but she wasn't sure Reed would like it. She toyed with the idea of making spaghetti, which was quick and pretty universal.

Half the spaghetti ingredients were on the granite kitchen counter when visions of a wildly romantic spaghetti dinner complete with wine, candles, garlic bread and salad assailed her. Marina froze with a large pot in her hands. She didn't want to give Reed the wrong impression. What's the right impression? she wondered idly as she placed the pot on the stove and put all the ingredients back into the refrigerator and cabinet except for the onions and green pepper. She had no answer for that question.

Opening her refrigerator again, Marina removed the chicken and salt pork, cured ham, chili peppers, tomatoes, chorizos and pimentos. Then she retrieved the oregano, garlic and rice from the cabinet. She was going to make her family's version of *asopao de pollo*.

With the soup cooking, Marina hurried into her room to find something to wear. "This is not a date. This is not a date," she repeated out loud as she went through all her clothes twice and found nothing suitable.

In desperation, she removed the suit she'd worn to work and hung it up. Then she found her best-looking jeans and pulled them on. With her full breasts and a tendency to sweat, she had to be careful what she wore on top. She pawed through tube tops and sleeve-less shells with visions of Reed trying not to stare at her chest all night. Finally she settled on a short-sleeved, striped cotton blouse. Stepping into her favorite sandals, she brushed her hair and pulled it into a ponytail.

Reed arrived at six forty-five with two bottles of soda and a bottle of wine. His eyes darkened as he took in her appearance appreciatively and stopped just short of staring. "You look different."

"Is that good or bad?"

"Good. Definitely good."

His words made her smile. "Come in," she said, re-membering her manners, "and let me take that bag."

"We don't have to drink the wine tonight since we'll be working," he explained.

"Of course not," she agreed, taking the bag and liking the silent implication that they would be together to drink it at another time. She thanked him for the beverages.

"I've got to get my briefcase and files from the car," he announced.

Glancing out the open entryway behind him, she saw that he'd left his car door ajar. "Do you need help?"

"No, I've got it." Reed turned and went back down the steps. He returned shortly with his briefcase and a stack of files. Closing the door, Marina showed him to the desk area she'd set up for them.

"Dinner smells good," he remarked, sniffing the air and looking around. "What is it?"

"*Asopao de pollo,* which is chicken soup." Marina eased some of her papers aside to give him more room. "I'm serving it with rice."

"Sounds good."

"I hope you like it," she responded, pulling out her chair and sitting.

Reed settled into his. "I can't imagine you cooking anything I wouldn't like."

Marina rolled her eyes. "Oh, now you're just shamelessly sucking up."

"Yeah, it was, wasn't it?" Reed asked, chuckling.

"We eat in about an hour," she announced.

"Then we'd better get started on our analysis," he

remarked. "Let's do potential victims first, since we're going to have to set up protection for them."

"Did you get pounded on that one, too?" Marina asked.

Reed nodded, opened a folder and pulled out a disc and a list. "Your disc or mine?"

"Mine. My computer's on and I have my spread-sheet up." She studied his list, which didn't look much different than her own. "So what do all the victims have in common besides Merriwhether and the Alpha Kappa Epsilon fraternity?"

"We already know that they shared a couple of classes. If necessary, we could get the class lists from Merriwhether. All were accused of rape or assault on the Merriwhether campus," Reed interjected.

Marina bit down on the top of her pen. "Were they all maybe guilty of assaulting the same female student?"

They checked through their respective piles of infor-mation. There were a couple of incidents where each of the victims so far had been accused of rape or assault. Reed's and Marina's gazes synched over the files. Had they found the most important link between the victims?

"Let's write this one down, note the names of victims and accused, and keep looking," she suggested. Her fingers were already typing the information into her spreadsheet.

Next they checked the rank order of the dates cited in the complaints against frat members against the order of the deaths. There was no visible correlation.

"Let's try something easy, like last names?" Reed

suggested, scanning his list. "If you went alphabetically, Russell, Edwards, Washington… No, it doesn't work."

Marina tapped her pencil on the desk. "How about Aubrey, Colton and Elliot? That's alphabetically correct and that's the order in which they were killed."

"Works for me! Put that on the spreadsheet," Reed said in a voice filled with energy.

When she was done, he asked, "So who's the next potential victim?"

She scanned her list. "Next three potential victims. Flint Huber, Gerry Chandler and Harrison Hicks, but I need to scrub this list again to make sure the names are right and that we've got all the contact information."

"Hey, Flint Huber is the alderman in my area," Reed noted. "Give me what you've got and I'll get it to the captain. He can assign a clerk to start the process of contacting them and arranging for protection."

"I think we've earned our dinner," Marina said as she finished typing in the last of their ideas. She printed a copy of the list and let Reed use her fax machine.

Washing her hands, she ladled soup and rice into bowls and put them on the table. She noticed that they'd actually worked an hour and a half. It was good that she'd kept the soup at a low simmer.

Reed washed his hands, too, found glasses and filled them with ice and soda.

They sat to eat in an atmosphere of warmth and easy camaraderie. She watched carefully, almost as if it were a sort of test as he tried the soup.

"Mmm, it's good." Reed nodded and began to eat with gusto.

Taking fresh air into her lungs, Marina realized that it had been a test of sorts. Despite the years she'd known Reed, she'd never cooked for him.

They ate, keeping up an easy flow of conversation. He made her laugh with a couple of jokes and a funny story about one of his partners. Afterward, she served fresh fruit salad and chocolate cake.

Reed ate heartily. "This is better than my mother's," he claimed, scarfing down his second piece of cake, "but if you tell her, I'll call you a liar."

Marina laughed and contented herself with the fruit salad. She'd already had more than enough of that chocolate cake.

Once the food was put away and the dishes done, they realized that it was getting late and they were tired. "I was looking forward to seeing what else we could come up with," she confessed as Reed gathered his files.

Reed shoved folders into his briefcase and snapped it shut. "Me, too. We can continue this in the morning."

She agreed.

Reed lingered, his hand on his briefcase.

In the expectant silence Marina held herself in check. If this had been a date she would have kissed him. Lord knew she wanted to. Professional behavior was ingrained in her, so she tried not to stare at his soft lips. "See you in the morning?" she asked finally.

For a split second he actually looked disappointed.

Recovering quickly he nodded and smiled. Then he thanked her for dinner and headed for the door.

Marina held the door open as he stepped out with his briefcase and files. Inches separated them but the heated energy of attraction between them made her heart race. She sucked in a deep breath.

In that moment their glances caught and held. What she saw in his eyes melted her insides. Pure unadulterated desire fueled the fire. On watery legs she leaned against the doorway, drowning in the no-man's-land between real and anticipated sensation and emotion.

He set the files on top of the briefcase and lifted a hand to smooth a loose strand of hair back from her face.

Trembling, she wet her lips.

"We did good tonight," he said in a husky voice.

"Yes," she murmured, riding the edge of excitement.

"Maybe even did enough to save Flint's life, huh?"

Swallowing, she didn't answer. Despite Reed's words about the task force, on a physical and emotional level they were really talking about something entirely different.

The telephone rang. Marina started, coming out of her daze. What was she doing lingering here with Reed?

He blinked, shifting his feet and regrouping as the phone continued to ring in a loud, annoying fashion that could not be ignored. "You'd better get that," he suggested finally.

"Yes." She forced her awkward limbs to work, praying she wouldn't trip and fall. Lifting the receiver she spoke into the phone, "Hello?"

"Marina?" Javier's voice filled her ears. "You sound funny. Are you okay?"

She cleared her throat. "Yes, Dad, I—I'm fine."

In the doorway Reed waved at her and turned to pull the door shut behind him.

"Let me call you back in a few minutes," she suggested, replacing the phone. Going to the window, she watched Reed get into his car and back out of her driveway. Then she went to the kitchen to fix herself a big glass of cold water. Drinking it with shaking fingers, she let herself acknowledge what had almost happened. If Reed had kissed her she would have fallen apart. Hell, she'd virtually fallen apart anyway. Gulping down the water she tried to cool off.

Still feeling a pleasant buzz from the celebration party for the new office building, Alderman Flint Huber enjoyed the night air, the breeze on his face, and let his imagination wander as to how the evening would end with his beautiful blond companion. The husky sweet sound of her voice sent chills through him and she was just this side of voluptuous with legs to die for and luscious lips. In the back of his thoughts he knew that somehow, somewhere, he'd seen her before, but how could he forget a woman like this?

At his side, but just a little in front of him, she pranced almost playfully in her heels, smiling coyly. He followed like a dog in heat, surprised when she stopped at the area where earlier today he'd help cut the ribbon signifying the start of construction.

"I want a private tour," she said, adding a low laugh.

He laughed, too, watching as she slipped into the loosely chained opening and picked her way across the dirt. He studied her ass, wondering if she was as toned as she looked beneath that sexy black dress.

She turned, lifting her skirt a little. "Coming?"

"Absolutely." Flint thought fleetingly of his driver who also doubled as security for him. He'd sent the man on an errand and promised to stay at the celebration until he returned. He realized that he should have let someone know where he was going, but then, he didn't want any witnesses to what was about to go down between him and his blond companion.

What was her name again? Carrie? Karen?

It doesn't matter anyway, Flint decided as he slipped through the gate. He figured that names had nothing to do with what they wanted from each other.

A hotel would have been better, but Flint wasn't quibbling since he liked to get a little freaky every now and then. One of those linen-covered tables or one of the soft mounds of dirt would make this memorable.

He caught up with her just inside the tent. She pulled him into a hot, wet kiss, her wild tongue making all sorts of promises. He slid a hand up her dress.

With a low laugh, she quickly moved away. "Drinks first."

Flint blinked in surprise. He hadn't seen her take anything from the celebration. "You brought something?"

"Mmm-hmm." She opened her bag to reveal two

small bottles of white wine. Twisting the caps off both, she offered him one.

He accepted and they both drank to his toast: "To good times."

Backing away from him, she scooted up on the linen-covered table, lifting one leg provocatively. When he started to follow, she stopped him. "No, you have to finish your drink first because I don't want any interruptions. Understand?" As if to show him how, she turned up her bottle and finished it.

With his eyes on the tantalizing view, Flint followed suit. Finishing, he almost dropped the bottle. He felt light-headed and a bit numb. He didn't remember drinking that much.

The blonde was on her side, beckoning him on with curled finger. He started toward her. It didn't quite go as he'd planned. His body moved, but his coordination was off. He stumbled.

"Come on, baby, show me what you've got," she taunted, still smiling.

He tried for a snappy answer, but his words were slurred. His mouth was dry, too, with a funny taste. He wondered what was happening to him. He hoped he'd still be able to sample the blonde.

Flint stumbled, and this time he fell. He tried to work his limbs. He couldn't get up.

"I'll come to you baby," the blonde said in the sweet, husky voice.

She leaned over him, smoothing the hair back from

his forehead. Then she fumbled with her bag. Something flashed in the moonlight filtering in from the front of the tent.

Flint's throat caught when he saw what it was. He tried to cry out but a painful, gruntlike sound was all he could manage.

The blonde's eyes were cold with malice. "This is for all of us, for what you did. You see you didn't really get away with it."

She fumbled with his belt and his pants. Then he saw the knife rise and come smashing down. Flint whimpered…

by ten and till get me something that says twelve. She was flustered, unable to catch her thought, even the train of thought.

"I've . . . " damn, "much what do you want to say . . . " and to prove her point, Marina said something to the effect of not knowing exactly what she was saying, but he was too . . . . [illegible]

"I've . . . " right now, we'll say your name . . . I don't know," it was her voice, but he was too . . . I mean, aren't you willing to . . . [illegible]

She smiled . . . a soft, sultry smile and had pulled her closer, and the . . . [illegible] . . . want of the moment.

Chapter 9

Reed was having a hell of a dream. They'd been having dinner when Marina shot him a dreamy-eyed looked then leaned over and kissed him. Now she was in his lap and all over him, hot, warm and sweet. He reveled in the taste of her mouth, her unique scent and the tactile feel of her soft curvy flesh in his arms.

A nagging, buzzing sound pulled at him. He fought it, realizing that he must be asleep. He didn't want to wake up.

Marina paused between kisses to rub her face against his and nibble his bottom lip. "Are you going to get that?"

Reed sat up in bed, pounding the mattress and cursing. Automatically, his gaze touched on the alarm clock he kept on the other side of the room. It was only five o'clock in the morning! His alarm wasn't ringing. It was the damned phone!

Lifting the receiver, he snarled a hello into the phone.

"Woke you up, huh?"

Reed recognized Marco's voice. He was a detective friend who worked the third shift. "You know you did, Dawg, so what's up?"

"We just found another mutilated body. This time it was Alderman Huber. We found him at the construction site for the new office building down on the waterfront. He was at the ribbon-cutting ceremony yesterday and came back later to party at the Yancy Street Hotel. Since the scene is still fresh, I figured you'd want to see it before the forensic boys get done and they pack things up."

"You figured right," he told Marco. "It sounds like something that should be handled by the task force anyway."

Copying the address on the pad he kept by the bed, Reed thanked Marco and put in a call to Marina.

Still half asleep, her voice was soft and melodious. As he'd suspected, she insisted on coming along and agreed to meet him at the site.

With a brief, brisk shower and some speed dressing, Reed was on his way.

At the construction site, a group of patrolmen kept people back. Reed flashed his badge and pulled Marina in along with him. When it looked as if there might be a problem, Marco appeared and vouched for them both.

At the tent, forensics had taken casts of high-heeled

footprints discovered where they'd found Huber, but they were a bit skeptical since many people had trampled the area during the ribbon-cutting ceremony. There was also a pointy high-heeled toe print in the blood near the body and forensics was busy capturing it.

Moving through the area in plastic-covered shoes and gloved hands, Reed and Marina stood outside the taped area taking in the scene.

Flint Huber was sprawled on the floor of tent with his pants and underwear down around his knees. He'd been stabbed and unmanned just like the other victims. Glassy-eyed in death, he stared up at them, his expression unnaturally calm.

Blood painted the scene, which was tainted with the stench of death. Reed swallowed bile. He heard Marina gag, but she, too, held onto the contents of her stomach. They stepped parallel to the line of yellow tape.

Scanning the area past the body, Reed noticed that the white-linen tablecloth on the nearby table was mussed and bore imprints that suggested that someone had been sitting on it.

"Flint Huber. He would have been next on the list if the rationale we worked out last night rings true," Reed noted.

"Only four more to go," Marina reminded him. "We've got to make sure protection is arranged for the rest of them."

Reed went back to watching forensics work. The science involved had always fascinated him. "You know this doesn't fit the four-month pattern, don't you?"

Marina sighed. "Yeah, I was thinking that, too. Maybe our killer saw an opportunity she couldn't pass up."

"Maybe." Reed inclined his head. "Or maybe she's changing the pattern."

"Dear Lord, I hope not," she said with a sigh. "We've got to stop her. I'm hoping we can bring her in alive."

Reed's gaze met hers. He didn't speak, but his expression spoke volumes. He thought she was dreaming.

Marina turned her attention back to where forensics was still painstakingly collecting evidence. "There's not much more we can do here. I'm going home to get another half hour of sleep and get ready for work," she announced.

When he didn't reply, she turned and started for her car. Reed fell into step beside her. Down near the gate, the patrolmen held a group of reporters at bay. They shouted questions at Reed and Marina.

"No comment," Reed called back calmly.

"Hey, I know you," one yelled as Marina went past. "You're not a cop, you're FBI. What are you doing here?"

"No comment." Marina kept walking.

When a group of reporters headed for them, she and Reed got into their cars and drove away.

Reed called Marina as soon as he got into his condo. "You know we're going to have to brief the press about the murders, don't you?"

Marina sounded tired. There was an undercurrent of irritability in her tone, probably because she hadn't got enough sleep. "Yeah, I knew it was coming. I just didn't think we had enough information about what's happened at the site to be briefing anyone."

"That's true, but I've seen how this works with other people assigned to task forces. We're going to have to brief the media and give them something to satisfy the public that we're working this. I'll see you in a couple of hours."

On the other end she responded quickly and hung up the phone. Reed didn't bother taking off his clothes to climb back into bed. He set the alarm clock and crashed on the couch, fully clothed.

By nine o'clock, the task force had received a direct request from the mayor to hold a press conference on their activities before the end of the day. The media now knew that Alderman Huber had been killed and a connection had been made to Elliot Washington's death.

Reed had been called in to brief his captain, Ean Shepherd, and Ross Spaulding, Marina's supervisor, had called for an update on their progress. Reed and Marina scheduled the briefing to the press for 3:00 p.m. to give forensics time to supply preliminary data, and themselves as much time as possible to prepare.

At three, Marina and Reed stood together at the wood podium in the station training room that had been converted into a briefing room for the press. She and Reed had drawn straws on who would speak first. She'd won. It hadn't been a popular decision with his management, but Reed had always been a straight-up guy. He stood by his decision and she loved him for it.

The room was filled with several local people she'd only seen on television before this. Working with Talbot, she been a part of national briefings to the press on several occasions, but standing here with Reed to brief on their work felt like a totally different game. She took in a breath and let it out slowly. As cameras flashed in their faces and cameramen jockeyed for optimum positions, she spoke into the microphone.

"Good afternoon," she began, pleased that her voice came out strong and confident. "I am FBI Special Agent Marina Santos of the National Center for the Analysis of Violent Crime and this is Lieutenant Reed Crawford of the Chicago Police Department. We're both co-chairs of the task force put together by the FBI and the Chicago Police Department at the request of Mayor Dansinger to identify and arrest what we believe to be a serial killer operating in the Chicago area. With the death of Alderman Flint Huber yesterday, we've identified four victims: Aubrey Russell, Colton Edwards, Elliot Washington and Flint Huber. Each victim was murdered, his body mutilated and left in a public place. Lieutenant Crawford will continue this briefing."

Marina stepped aside and Reed took his place in front of the microphone and reintroduced himself.

"As part of our investigation, we've been working to

determine what the victims have in common and if the killer is selecting them at random. We have established that the choice of victims is not random. Each victim has been between the ages of twenty-six to twenty-eight. Each victim attended Chicago's Merriwhether University during the same three-year period and all belonged to certain organizations that we are not prepared to identify at this time. We are in the process of contacting potential victims and offering them protection. We're asking that anyone with information about any of these murders, that could lead to an arrest, please contact the taskforce at 1-800-TForce1. This concludes our briefing. We will now have a short question and answer period."

Justin Cleary of the local ABC station got his question in first. "Should all male students who attended Merriwhether during the years the current victims attended be worried? How big is your pool of potential victims?"

"No, all male students at the college during the years the victims attended should not be worried," Reed answered from his place at the podium. "We've identified a much smaller group at risk and are currently notifying them of the danger and making arrangements for their safety."

Carla Corbin, another reporter at a local station followed up with the next question. "What are you doing for former students at risk who may have moved out of the area?"

"We're asking male former students who attended Merriwhether with the victims and belonged to the same organizations on campus to contact the task force if the information on file with Merriwhether is not current."

"Are we looking for a male or female serial killer?" Ron Collins, a *Tribune* reporter interjected.

"The evidence to date indicates that the killer is a woman," Marina said.

Collins nodded in response.

The next question came from a *Chicago Sun Times*' reporter who was always critical of the police and other law enforcement agencies. "How long has the task force been working these murders?"

"A little over three weeks," Marina responded, straightening her shoulders and bracing for a healthy dose of criticism.

"If you knew that a select group of Merriwhether students was in danger from a serial killer, why didn't you warn the public? Maybe you could have saved Alderman Huber's life."

Marina faced the reporter, fighting hard to keep the anger out of her voice. "Actually, we didn't identify the group until yesterday and it could still be a coincidence. We suspected that former Merriwhether students were in danger, but we could not be certain which group until we gathered and analyzed enough evidence. Starting a wholesale panic among the former students was contrary to the public interest."

"How many potential victims remain?"

"We are not prepared to make that information public at this time," Reed said, giving Marina time to recover her temper.

"How big is your task force?" an older man in the back row called.

"Special Agent Santos has access to all FBI resources needed and I have access to all the C.P.D. resources," Reed answered diplomatically.

"So there's just the two of you!" the man stressed.

Reed ignored him.

"Last question," Marina announced, checking the clock with anticipation. She selected a slender, nondescript female reporter from one of the smaller newspapers. "What are your and Lieutenant Crawford's qualifications for running a task force?"

Marina all but let out a sigh of relief. This question would be easy. "I've worked in the FBI's Center for the Analysis of Violent Crime for a number of years, most of it working to bring down high-profile serial killers with Lowell Talbot. Lieutenant Crawford has spent a number of years with C.P.D. working high-profile cases in homicide and honing his investigative skills."

"Why isn't Talbot working this one?" the reporter retorted. "Doesn't Chicago merit the best the FBI and the C.P.D. have to offer?"

Heat burned the surface of the skin on Marina's face and neck. That comment was a particular twist of the knife in her gut. She'd worked hard to get to the place where she would be offered an assignment like this and she was damned and determined to do her job. She ground her teeth, swallowing back bitter words that could be twisted and misinterpreted by the press.

While she struggled with herself, Reed spoke in a calm, authoritative voice. "Both agencies feel that Ms. Santos and I have the skills necessary to stop this killer."

Marina recovered. "This concludes our briefing. Thank you all for coming."

More camera flashes, a few more questions tossed out for comment and ignored, and then it was over.

"Not bad," Captain Shepherd declared from the back of the room when the last of the press had gone. "Of course there'll be more fallout over Huber, so get ready. He was popular with the press. The sooner you bring down this serial killer, the better."

Reed and Marina gathered their things and walked back to their office. They barely looked at each other. Marina felt as if she'd been through an emotional wringer.

Inside the office, the temp they'd left working the phones was busy. She'd already received several calls from former Merriwhether students. Two of them were students on Reed and Marina's potential victim list. They'd been asked to come into the station, but had elected to wait until tomorrow. They had requested increased patrols in their areas and agreed to stay home.

Marina was determined to go home and rest. The press conference had been draining. In addition, she figured that she had at least a little downtime before the killer struck again. In fact she could almost imagine the killer in a room somewhere laughing at how she'd gotten away with another murder.

On the way out, Marina and Reed passed the break area where several cops were gathered around the wall-mounted television. On the screen was a replay of a portion of the press conference they'd conducted earlier. A scathing review of the press conference and the task force work being done by Reed and Marina followed. Mercifully, someone changed the channel, but the new station featured more of the same. When another station change yielded the same refrain, Reed and Marina turned and headed for their cars.

"If you listen to them, we're the most incompetent pair on the planet," Reed mused darkly as they went through the gate to the parking lot.

"It'll get better," Marina said, determined to rise above this round of negativity. "We can get together and work on our list of perpetrators. Maybe something will pop out of it."

"Not tonight." Reed cut her off. "I need a task force break tonight and I figure it'll have to last me for a while."

Marina swallowed and said good night. Normally she would have argued with him or bullied him into seeing that they had to work together and push on, but she was still feeling too bruised from the way things had turned out. She knew that the media attack and the day's events were just temporary setbacks, but in truth, Reed's words echoed thoughts she'd been trying to suppress.

Marina's mind was all but numb from overwork and

stress. She felt overwhelming guilt for not moving through the case information fast enough to stop another murder and yet, what could she have done? She and Reed had worked hard. Damned hard. Marina had come under fire while working with Lowell Talbot, but never like this. Talbot had somehow known how to play the media like an instrument. They'd loved him.

She glanced back at Reed, noting that he'd assumed that calm, brick-hard expression that covered a multitude of emotions. He'd had that expression when she'd dumped him, too. Why couldn't she forget about that?

On automatic pilot, Marina got in her car and drove. She didn't want to go home where her family and friends would be sure to drop by or to call to hash over the news reports. She oscillated between thoughts of going to the gym to hit the punching bag and drowning her sorrows at the bar.

The gym won. She changed and went a good forty minutes with the punching bag. Afterward, she showered and put on fresh clothing, but replays of the press conference still weighed her down. Worst of all, the nagging realization that the serial killer had changed the mode of operation hovered like a dark cloud. Anything could happen now, even another murder.

Chapter 10

Somehow Marina ended up at Cuff's, the local cop hangout. She sat at the corner end of the black leather bar and drowned her sorrows in a couple of Black Russians.

As she sipped the second drink, she saw Reed seated three stools down from her. He was staring into space morosely, a whiskey glass to his lips and an empty one in front of him.

Briefly she toyed with the idea of joining him. Had he seen her and decided to drink alone? She realized that she really didn't care because the prospect of hurting with Reed was a damned sight better than sitting here hurting alone.

Marina stood on unsteady feet. Those Black Russians

were stronger than she'd thought. Holding her drink, she moved down.

"Great minds think alike," she said, taking the stool next to Reed.

He glanced at her briefly. "We're in the same hole."

"We'll get out of this. We'll find our serial killer," she assured him.

"That's for damned sure." He stared down into his drink as if it held all the answers. "I remember something Mom used to say a lot. Be careful what you wish for, you might get it. You've been through this before. What could we have done to come out smelling like roses?"

Shaking her head, she swallowed the last of her drink. "There was no way for us to be heroes unless we'd already caught the killer. We can't find our killer through the media."

Reed's somber gaze touched her. "It's been done."

Shifting on her stool, she ordered yet another drink. "Yes, but we couldn't have given them everything we've worked out. Too much is at stake."

"Not to mention the sterling reputations of our fine pool of potential victims," he added sarcastically.

Marina didn't have a comeback for that. She had more than enough inner conflict over protecting the slimy group of young men who more likely than not were being stalked by one of their past victims. She sipped the rest of her drink silently.

By ten, they were both plastered though they'd stopped drinking to consume a couple of burgers. Reed stood slowly. "We should go."

Holding on to the counter, Marina stood, too. "I can't drive like this."

"I'm tired of this joint," Reed said, his words slurring only slightly. "You can come by, have some coffee, and come back when you've sobered up. You know I don't stay too far."

Giggling, Marina covered her mouth. She wasn't normally a woman who giggled. "How are we going to get there? Did you drive, too?"

"I walked. I do that sometimes, just to work off stress." Reed straightened. He studied the crowd. "I'll get us a ride."

She saw him talking to someone at the bar and then the bartender. Several minutes later a taxi dropped them off at Reed's. Glancing around, Marina spared a brief thought for Reed's stalker as she followed him upstairs and into his loft apartment.

The first thing that grabbed her attention was the group of framed photos on the wall in the entryway. The center featured an enlarged photo of their college friends at last year's Christmas party. She'd been hanging with Reed that night and having a blast. Her glorious smile in that picture haunted her. She hadn't been that happy since.

Reed closed and locked the door behind her. "Coffee?"

"Please." She followed him across the hardwood

floor into the modern kitchen. While he started making the coffee, she sat slumped at the counter, watching him.

He moved slow and deliberately, but was still a bit unsteady on his feet. He looked handsome in a rough, Reed sort of way. If he felt like she did right now, it was much easier to sit or lie down.

"I appreciate you helping me out," she said.

"No problem. You'd do the same for me."

"Yeah, but I think you'd get instant. I'm not for moving too much right now."

He chuckled. "I guess you're just lucky."

She giggled. Damn, she wished she could stop that. "Yeah, I am lucky. I think a man working out in the kitchen is just too damned sexy."

"Truth?" His tone dipped a bit.

"Oh, *yeah.*" Sucking on her bottom lip, she eyed him with what she hoped was a come-and-get-me look. It was an invitation and a challenge.

It must have worked. Reed pushed the button on the automatic coffeemaker and headed for her.

She was almost breathless with anticipation when he got there.

"I've been wanting to kiss you," he muttered, settling in the chair beside her and pulling her close.

The scent of him mixed with whiskey and cologne filled her nostrils, making her dizzy. "I've been wanting you to kiss me," she admitted, tilting her head up.

He leaned down and his mouth fastened on hers in a warm, tantalizing swirl of lips, tongue and Reed. Marina plunged into the depths of sensation. Thrusting her fingers into his thick hair and massaging the sides of his face and neck, she tried to get even closer.

His hands slid restlessly up and down her back as he pressed her so close that the aching tips of her breasts burned hot against his chest. She was half in her seat and half in his lap. He deepened the kiss.

A tremor went through him and echoed one within her. She moaned in pleasure.

Reed moved away, pushing her securely back into her seat.

"No," she protested breathlessly.

"Coffee's ready," he said firmly. Reed pushed to his feet and headed for the coffeemaker.

That's when the full-bodied fragrance of it hit her nostrils. Marina sagged against the counter, still hungry for Reed and his kisses.

He opened cabinets and drawers, producing mugs, spoons, sugar, artificial sweetener and caramel-nut-flavored creamer.

While he fixed the coffee, she closed her eyes, working to get past mounting frustration. She was used to working for what she wanted and getting it. Why couldn't she have Reed? Surely he'd had time to get past her mistake in choosing Emilio over him.

Reed approached the counter with a tray. He set a steaming cup of coffee in front of her.

"Here. Drink this."

Pushing up on her elbows, she breathed in its aroma.

Her mouth watered, but she really wasn't up to drinking anything so hot.

As if reading her thoughts, he gave her a spoon. "You can start with this."

"So my kisses turn you off?" she asked lazily, stirring her coffee and sipping a couple of spoonfuls.

His eyes narrowed. "You know better than that."

"So what gives?"

He gave her the you're-so-stupid look. "If you weren't so pickled, you'd know. We're both drunk. What seems like a good idea now could be something we'll both regret tomorrow."

"I know what I want," she insisted.

"Really? Then let's talk when we're both sober, 'cause I'm not taking you up on anything tonight."

The nerve of him. She sipped her coffee in silence, burning up inside.

"Quit pouting," he admonished, drinking his coffee across from her and running a hand over his face.

"I'm not pouting."

"Yes, you are. You do it whenever you don't get what you want." He chuckled.

"No, I don't," she insisted, pulling in her drooping bottom lip.

He didn't bother with a reply. When she was done with her coffee, he led her into his great room and sat next to her on the black leather sofa.

Marina leaned over to place her head on the armrest. The room was spinning.

"I'm not up to getting the car right now," he said. "All I can think about is my bed. It's been a long night. Think we could just get up early to pick up your car?"

"Sure." She wondered if he'd changed his mind about being with her.

Abruptly, Reed hauled her to him for another soul stirring, toe-curling kiss. They were both breathless when he pulled away.

"I'll get you a pillow and some sheets," he choked out in a low tone.

Disappointed, Marina didn't bother to respond. She wasn't going to beg. Closing her eyes, she rode the waves of sensation still simmering inside her from his kiss. She barely felt him lift her head to place a pillow beneath it and covering her with a blanket.

"Good night, Marina."

She felt his soft lips on her forehead. Then he was gone.

At 4:00 a.m. Marina awakened. She was not in her bed. It took a few seconds to remember that she was at Reed's and why. She toyed with the idea of walking down the hall to join him in the king-size bed. She hadn't been so drunk that she didn't remember him rejecting her. Instead she got up and went into the bathroom to freshen up as best she could.

As she stepped out of the bathroom she heard him call her name. Turning back in the dim illumination from the night-light, she caught a glimpse of tousled hair and naked chest. Reed looked good enough to fuel a thousand fantasies.

"Give me fifteen minutes and I'll drive you to your car," he promised.

Twenty minutes later, he dropped her off at Cuff's. The bar had been closed for hours, but her car was fine. Reed had apparently asked one of his buds on duty to keep an eye on it.

"Thanks for taking care of me," she murmured, covering his hand briefly with hers.

"Anytime. It was a pleasure," he said, those brown eyes speaking volumes.

The problem was that Marina didn't know how to interpret what she saw in them. She scooted across the seat and got out. "See you at work in a few."

He echoed the sentiment as she closed the door.

Marina drove home thinking Reed Crawford was a true-blue knight. It was one of the things she loved most about him. He'd taken care of her when she was vulnerable and gone out of his way to avoid taking advantage. Her mind replayed scenes from their evening together and a smile spread across her face. Somehow, some way, she would clear the air with him and see if he still had the same feelings for her.

Chapter 11

Blinking behind her darkest sunglasses in the bright morning sunlight, Marina arrived at work determined to move the task force forward.

Javier had been camped out on her couch when she'd arrived home and she'd had difficulty evading his questions. She'd finally had to resort to ignoring them. It made her feel bad because she'd always had a close relationship with her father and she respected his opinion and his feelings. But he needed to acknowledge that she was an adult. Her problem was that her feelings for Reed were still too undefined for her to let anyone else in on their existence.

Javier had looked a little sad. Once he'd realized that she wasn't going to give him the details of her evening out, he'd focused on the press conference. Astute enough to know how the bad press had affected her, he told her how proud he was to have her as his daughter and how much good she did with her work. When he finished she felt comforted.

"I love you Dad," she'd said as he hugged her hard and turned his head to kiss her cheek.

Javier had given her his thousand-watt smile. "Love you, too, *mija*."

He'd insisted on making her toast while she readied for work, and stayed to make sure she ate some of it. He'd taken off when she left for work.

Marina slowed her walk and lengthened her stride once she discovered that each step caused a sharp answering pain in her head. At any other time she would have called in sick, but she'd be damned if she let anyone at the FBI or C.P.D. tack on the name coward to what was already being said in the media.

In the empty task force office, Marina settled at her desk with a bunch of typed sheets the temp had left. The woman was good, Marina thought as she scanned the pages. The temp had gotten the contact information from the potential victims who had called in and checked them against the Merriwhether records and Reed and Marina's task force lists. In addition, she'd contacted the other two former students and arranged for all of them to come in for a ten o'clock meeting with the task force.

Walking slow and carefully, Reed arrived with an

orange juice jug filled with a reddish orange concoction. Producing two ten-ounce paper cups from a bag, he filled them with the liquid and offered her one.

"What is it?" she asked, eyeing it suspiciously.

"Mom's cure for hangovers." Reed lifted his cup and drained it in one long, continuous series of gulps.

"And what's in it?"

"Some of everything, so don't ask." He tossed his empty cup into the trash. "All I can say is that it works. You'll feel better in half an hour, guaranteed."

Marina's stomach whined. She'd tried to eat toast at home, but her mouth and throat had been too dry to swallow much. Water hadn't helped. Coming to a decision, she lifted her cup and followed Reed's example. The concoction wasn't as bad as she'd imagined. She was sick enough to want to drink it.

"Half an hour and you'll feel fine," Reed promised again.

Marina showed him the information the temp had gathered and told him about the ten o'clock appointment. Together they studied the list of remaining potential victims: Gerry Chandler, Harrison Hicks, John Stuart and Marshall Mason.

"If the killer goes the way she's been going, Gerry's at the top of her list," Marina remarked.

Reed nodded in agreement.

At ten, the former students arrived and Reed moved the group to a bigger office for the meeting. Marina followed, already beginning to feel better. She was going to have to ask Trudy for the recipe for her concoction.

Inside the office, Marina studied each of the young men curiously. She knew that being accused of rape and assault didn't make a person guilty, but based on the information she and Reed had gathered, the odds weren't in favor of their innocence.

Gerry Chandler was a tall, lanky man with freckles, rust-colored hair and sea-green eyes. He seemed friendly enough and not at all embarrassed that he needed police protection due to something he might have done during his time at Merriwhether. He was an environmental analyst at GTC—Global Terraforming Cooperative Corporation.

A financial analyst, Harrison Hicks was about five foot eleven with blue eyes, a sensual mouth and a head full of dark shiny hair that he'd pulled back and tied with a cord. Women would have killed for his creamy skin and long thick eyelashes. Hell, Marina thought, he'd have made a pretty woman. Quiet and subdued, he seemed aware that his looks attracted a lot of attention. He didn't look like a man who would have to rape anyone, but then Marina knew that rape wasn't about the sex. It was about control.

Harrison sat quietly with the group, listening to their banter and responding to questions, but Marina sensed something odd or different about him.

John Stuart, a leading cryptographer with the department of defense, had a short, stocky build, sandy-brown hair and brown eyes. He cordially recognized the others, but more or less kept his distance. Behind his bland expression Marina detected a bit of distaste.

This was more along the lines of what she'd expected to see. She imagined, too, that the serial killer and the need for police protection was wrecking havoc with all their lives.

Marshall Mason was last and a few minutes late for the meeting. A gemologist, he had curly black hair, lively gray eyes and a gregarious manner.

Introducing Marina and himself, Reed started the meeting by reviewing the information they'd gathered on the serial killer and explaining that membership in the Alpha Kappa Epsilon fraternity, being the subject of on-campus rape or assault allegations, and attending Merriwhether during a specific three-year period had likely landed each of them on the serial killer's list. He told them that Elliot had a meeting scheduled with an unknown woman the night he'd died, and that witnesses had seen Alderman Huber leaving the new construction celebration party with an unknown woman, and Reed suspected something similar happened with Aubrey Russell, who had been found behind a popular night-club. If they were going to survive, they had to be careful not to go out alone or to go off with strangers until the serial killer had been caught.

"Who's next on the list?" Marshall asked when there was a lull in the conversation.

"As near as we can determine, it's Gerry," Marina

said. She didn't believe in holding her punches. "This information isn't something to be shared with the press. We'll do what we can to protect you."

Gerry's forehead wrinkled and his shoulders slumped. A troubled expression marred his young face. "How long do I have before she makes a run for me?"

This was a question that Marina had spent a lot of time thinking about. She answered Gerry carefully. "We'd gauged it at about four months between murders, but Alderman Huber's murder threw all of that out of the window. If I had to guess, I'd say you're okay for a couple of weeks, but beyond that…"

Marshall's boyish voice rang out in the stunned silence. "And who's on the list after Gerry?"

Reed turned to meet Harrison Hicks' gaze. "Harrison."

"Why me, then Harrison?" Gerry asked hoarsely.

"Because the killer seems to be going in alphabetical order," Marina answered.

"For the record, I'm innocent," Marshall said, anger creeping into his voice. "I never did anything to any stupid bitch who wasn't willing."

The others shot him traitorous looks. Marina's eyes narrowed.

"We're innocent, too," Harrison stormed in a tone that made Marina wish she could read his mind. "We proved our innocence in court."

With that farce of a trial? She didn't say it out loud, but Marina noticed that none of them could meet her gaze. "Right now, what the serial killer thinks is the only thing that matters," she snapped.

Reed's lips formed a straight line. He pushed on in a grim tone. "We'll start by keeping up the increased patrols in your areas. We want you to check in with us regularly and report anything suspicious. This is also the time to stay away from strangers and any of the women who went to Merriwhether, at least until this thing is over with."

The other men nodded.

"With the limited resources we have, we're focusing on Gerry," Marina explained, "but we're making the most of undercover support for the rest of you, so at any given time you could be under surveillance."

As the meeting ended, Reed and Marina planned to get back to Gerry with a schedule and pledged to stay in contact with the others.

Marina felt as if they were moving forward again. She would spend the rest of the afternoon scrubbing the list of possible killers.

As the others got up and left, Harrison hung back, insisting on speaking to them alone. They closed the door once more.

"You know that I was the one who found Aubrey after those women attacked him on campus years ago?" he began, looking a little pale.

"Yes. We have that information in the files," Marina assured him.

Harrison's eyes took on a faraway look. "I saw them

running away. If I hadn't showed up, they would have killed him."

What he said was true. Marina had seen the police report and the pictures in the file.

"One of the women got time in jail and two years probation," Reed noted. "They never identified the other."

"Yeah, but have you checked her alibi for the night Aubrey and the others were killed?" A note of fear crept into his voice.

"We've been chasing other leads, but I'll check on this woman's alibis today," Marina promised.

Harrison ran a hand that trembled just a little through his hair. "I guess I've got a little time if Gerry's next," he murmured.

Reed put a hand on Harrison's shoulder. "We're going to catch this killer before anyone else gets killed."

"Well, I'm counting on you to catch the killer, Lieutenant." Harrison's voice was dangerously close to a sob. After about a minute he turned and went for the door. "I gotta go."

Neither Reed nor Marina spoke as Harrison's footsteps echoed down the hall. They gathered their notes and things and started back to the task force office.

"That Harrison is kind of strange," Marina noted.

Reed inclined his head. "Yeah, I thought the same thing, too, but he's probably more scared than anything. Out of all of them he's the last one I'd pick as the perpetrator of any violent activity."

"That's for sure." Inserting her key into the lock,

she opened the door to the task force office and stepped inside.

Reed followed. "Have you got an address on the woman who attacked Aubrey?"

Plopping down in her office chair, she riffled through her files. "Her name was Jasmine O'Leary. I've got an old one from the university, but it's probably no good. Her probation officer is bound to have a current one. Let's find out who it is and see."

Luck was with them this time because they ran a police computer search on Jasmine O'Leary's name and came up with a new address and her probation officer's name.

Marina studied Jasmine's picture. The woman had movie star looks and a wiry, well-proportioned build. Before she'd done six months in jail, she'd had a major role in a play at the university theater. Noting the determined angle of Jasmine's chin and the fearless look in her eyes, Marina wondered if nearly killing Aubrey Russell had satisfied her need for revenge. Could Jasmine be on a twisted rampage of justice and revenge? And if she was, she'd surely learned better ways to cover her tracks during her prison stint.

Marina's brows furrowed. She and Reed would have to tread very carefully with Jasmine O'Leary.

Chapter 12

It was lunchtime and for once Marina wasn't even thinking of food. She and Reed were in Forest Park where Jasmine O'Leary stayed and worked as the manager of Bailey's, a retail clothing store.

Marina walked into the store and immediately recognized Jasmine where she stood behind the counter talking to a customer. She had added a flattering amount of weight to her wiry, five-foot-eleven build. The short black suit complimented the blond hair she'd pinned up. Her gaze intensified, recognition and resignation dawning in her blue eyes. "I'll be with you in a minute," she said pleasantly.

Marina used the time to look through the sections of clothes for a cocktail dress. She hadn't bought anything sexy since her promotion. The rack filled with vibrant red, pink, fuchsia and blue caught her attention. Her closet already brimmed with colorful things. With thoughts of trying to be more conservative, she went through the rack of little black dresses first. One with a side split and a diagonal cutout across the breasts caught her eye and she held it up in the light.

Reed shook his head. "Nice, but you know that's not you," Reed said.

"How do you know I haven't changed?" she retorted.

"You haven't," he said with authority. With that, he rummaged through the stands filled with colorful gowns. He pulled out a red halter dress with a dropped waist and handkerchief skirt.

Tilting her head, Marina shot him a look of surprise. It was exactly what she'd been looking for. Now what do you do with a man like that? she wondered. In her innermost thoughts she'd been having dreams of letting their time together extend past the time they spent working on the task force. She'd been thinking of keeping him.

"That gown would look wonderful on you." Jasmine spoke from just behind Marina.

The chime on the door rang as the other customer opened the door and left the shop.

Jasmine's gaze rested on Marina. "You're not really here to shop, are you?"

"No." Marina stepped away from the rack of dresses. "I'm Special Agent Marina Santos and this is Lieutenant Reed Crawford of the Chicago Police Department. We need to talk to you about what you were doing two nights ago."

Sighing, Jasmine drew her shoulders back. "You mean, the night that Flint Huber got himself killed?"

Reed replaced the red dress and rounded the racks of clothing. "That's exactly what we mean."

Jasmine's lips tightened. "I was wondering how long it would take you to get to me. I saw both of you on the news last night. Did you know that I was raped at a campus party by a couple of guys from Alpha Kappa Epsilon?" Her tone increased in volume. "One of them was Aubrey Russell, and he put something in my drink. Yes, a friend and I tried to even the score by beating him up. I've always been good with my fists. I know now that I should have taken my chances in court."

Marina met her angry gaze. "Did you kill Aubrey Russell?"

Jasmine shook her head. "No, but I'm not surprised or sorry someone else did. He took something that can't be replaced and I will never, ever be the same."

"Where were you the night before last?" Reed asked.

"I went to the Scream concert with my friend Kara. I've got ticket stubs, drink receipts, and it didn't end until two in the morning," she answered in an energy-filled voice. "My friend can verify that I didn't leave early."

Reed named the date that Elliot had been killed and asked for Jasmine's alibi.

Her forehead wrinkled as she tried to remember,

then her tension dissolved in a smile. "I got a new boy-friend. That was our first night together. His name is Dustyn Fogerty."

"What about the night Aubrey Russell was killed?" Marina asked, naming the date.

"I think I was out with friends. You can't expect me to remember everything just like that," Jasmine complained.

"But it's not just like that, is it?" Marina pushed. "You said you were wondering how long it would take us to get to you. If that's true, why wouldn't you spend time thinking about what you'd say when we got here?"

Jasmine simply shook her head. "I'm giving you the truth. I spent six months in prison because of Aubrey Russell and my own stupidity. Why would I give him more than he's already taken?"

"Maybe going to prison made you that much more determined to get him for good," Reed suggested.

"So why would I wait so long to go after them?"

Marina slanted Jasmine a glance. "Six months in prison and two years of probation—add a couple of months to make sure you're not being watched and the timing is perfect."

Jasmine's chin came up. "That's not how it is with me. I'll give you the names, addresses and phone numbers for Dustyn and my friends to verify my alibi. Other than that, I can't help you. I *didn't* kill anyone."

The facts they'd gathered had been going 'round and 'round in Marina's head for days. Now they were be-ginning to settle into a pattern. She moved closer, studying Jasmine's face. "Who was the woman who helped you attack Aubrey Russell at Merriwhether?"

Jasmine froze for a few startling moments. Her mouth opened and closed. "I…don't remember."

Marina expelled her breath in an incredulous huff. "You don't remember the woman who helped you beat the crap out a man who raped you? A woman who got away with it and no jail time? I don't believe it."

"It was someone new to the crisis center and she didn't come back after that."

"So what did she look like?"

"Average everything."

"What color hair?"

"Brunette?"

"You mean, she wasn't blond?" Reed asked in a tone that implied he might know more.

"I—I really don't remember." Jasmine looked scared.

"What are you hiding? Who are you trying to protect?" Marina asked, pressuring her.

"I'm not hiding anything. I'm not protecting anyone, either." Jasmine covered her face with her hands. "I paid for my crime. Can't you all just leave me alone?"

Marina lowered her tone. "Not until we get what we came for."

"We need everything you've got to support your alibis for the night of each murder and the contact information for you friends," Reed explained.

"Okay." Sniffling, Jasmine dropped her hands. Her eyes were damp.

Reed and Marina shared a glance as Jasmine went to the counter to write out the information. That's when Marina realized that they'd been playing good cop/bad cop. She'd always known that they'd make a good team.

Jasmine agreed to drop the rest of her information by the station in the morning. If she couldn't find her ticket stubs, Marina knew she could check with the credit card company.

"Do you remember the name of the woman who used to run the crisis center on campus?" Marina asked idly as she and Reed prepared to leave.

Jasmine nodded, some of the animation returning to her face. "Elizabeth Hatcher. She was good. She made us all realize that we were not powerless, and not just people in the crisis center. Ms. Hatcher counseled and worked with some of the groups formed through the Student Advocate Office."

Marina's eyes narrowed. "Didn't Hatcher counsel the group you were in with the woman who helped you beat Aubrey Russell?"

Jasmine's fingers closed around the ink pen so tightly that her knuckles were white. "Yes," she said in a barely audible tone.

"And you still can't remember your helper's name?" Reed interjected.

"No." Jasmine shook her head. "No."

"Jasmine, we'll check your alibis and let you know when and if you're clear," Reed said as they wrapped up the interview. Lowering his voice, he turned to

Marina, inclining his head. "I think you should buy the dress."

Something in his voice sent a fission of heat shimmering through her. "Really? So do I," she quipped. Opening her bag, she reached for her wallet.

Once they were back in the car, Marina faced Reed and said, "The more I hear about Elizabeth Hatcher, the more I know we need to talk to her. She was heading the group at Merriwhether when the women attacked Aubrey. I'm betting that she knows who the other woman was. We're talking about someone who helped beat the man enough to put him in a hospital. We don't know her story, but it could easily cover enough for her to go after all those men. After what happened with Huber, we've got to jump on this as soon as we can. We're going after Hatcher first thing in the morning."

Chapter 13

Reed pulled into the lot of a little Italian restaurant.

Marina's hand went to her stomach. She had been feeling a little weak. Forgetting to eat was unusual for her, but the truth was that she had been totally absorbed in solving the case.

The restaurant looked like something Marina had dreamed up. The waiter wore a black suit with a white shirt and bow tie. The small cozy tables were linen-covered and featured bottles of wine, crystal wine-glasses and intimate candle lighting. Romantic music played in the background.

Reed's and Marina's glances met and held. Reed shrugged. "Hey, people have been telling me about this place for a long time. I just thought we'd try it."

Marina didn't believe that for a minute. She guessed that this was Reed's answer to dating her without dating her, and she liked it. Their table sat in a semiprivate little alcove. Smiling, she opened her menu and immediately saw what she wanted in the list of entrées: chicken cacciatore.

They ordered food and a glass of wine each. Since it was almost three in the afternoon, Marina reasoned that they were probably done for the day. While they sipped their wine they stared at each other. The energy between them was so strong that Marina couldn't stop thinking about how it had felt to kiss Reed.

"Remember our bet?" he prompted with a smile.

Damn, that silly bet. She felt the blood rush to her face. Why had she bet Reed that the Alpha Kappa Epsilon fraternity would not be the link between the victims? It had been a sucker bet. Granted there were other links, but this was a major one.

Marina wet her lips. "What do you want?"

Speculation lit his eyes and sent her pulse racing. She'd said that she wouldn't sleep with him. Now she knew it had been a lie.

"Reed?" Marina prompted, forcing herself to breathe.

His eyes darkened. "A kiss. I want a kiss."

"Yes," she whispered. She wanted it, too.

They shared a smile as he leaned across the little table, his face inching closer and closer. Again, the heat rushed her face. She felt it spread, inside and out. When his warm hands touched her wrists and slid up her arms in a massaging motion, her lids drifted shut.

His warm, soft lips touched hers, enveloping them and invoking a fluttery tingle of sensation that spread through her and made her yearn to immerse herself in him. She tilted her face up, silently begging for more.

Deepening the kiss, Reed slipped his tongue between her lips. With a heartfelt sigh, Marina reveled in the dizzying taste of Reed and red wine. They pulled apart reluctantly.

Abruptly the sound of the background music and the low buzz of conversation in the restaurant rushed back at her. She and Reed stared at each other, silently acknowledging that sometime, somewhere, there would be a lot more to follow the kiss.

The waiter brought their food. They began to eat, still maintaining that invisible connection.

"We need to talk," she murmured between delicious bites of food. She'd come to a decision.

"About last night?" His tone pulled at something deep inside her.

She slanted a glance. "I understand last night and I'm not drunk now. Neither are you. I want to talk about last year."

Something flickered in his eyes and was gone before she could name it. "I don't. Let's enjoy the moment."

Sooner or later she was going to have to say it. Marina hated apologies. She'd been gathering her courage ever since she realized that she falling for Reed again.

"I—I want to apologize for how I ended things last year."

"You've already apologized for that," he reminded her.

"Then I want to explain."

"It's all in the past." He sipped from his glass. "Do you have to?"

"Yes." She sensed that he was waiting. "I love my family," she began. "You know we're very close."

Reed nodded.

"You know that I spend a lot of time with them, too." She met his gaze, silently asking for understanding. "Last year was extra special for me because I was dating Emilio and you, and crazy about you both. I should have just let things play out, but you know me, I charge ahead and fix things afterward." Stopping to gauge his reaction, she gleaned nothing except the feeling he was uncomfortable. She charged on. "I—I couldn't pick between the two of you on my own, so I considered other things and what others liked and thought."

"Nice to know I stood out in the crowd," he quipped.

Marina winced. She was making a mess of this.

"And?" he prompted, setting his glass on the table.

"Emilio was a family friend who spoke Spanish, and they liked him a lot. Of course they liked you, too, but…"

"He had the shared heritage thing going on?"

Marina nodded. "Yes, but once you were out of the picture I realized that he wasn't the one for me."

"So why didn't you come back for another chance with me?"

An uncomfortable pressure settled about her neck and shoulders, weighing her down. It had to do with her pushing herself to make this explanation and anticipating Reed's reaction. She wet her lips and swallowed. "I didn't come back because I'd already hurt you. I didn't know if you'd forgive me and then I went through a period where I didn't know what I wanted."

"And now you do?" His voice dipped lower, his eyes darkening.

"Yeah. I want another chance with you, Reed, and it doesn't matter what anybody else thinks."

Reed's expression was a stubborn combination of hurt and anger. "I don't know if that's a good idea."

"Yes, you do." Reaching across the table, she caught his hand. "You can be mad at me, go ahead, but if you're honest with yourself, you won't turn away."

"So now you're telling me how to act when you're the one who dropped me?" Reed's voice rang with so much emotion it made her heart ache.

"Yes, because I love you. Reed, I'm sorry!" Tears slipped down her cheek. She realized that she was crying. Marina rarely cried. Dropping her head in supreme embarrassment, she concentrated on making the tears stop.

Reaching out with his fingertips, he gently wiped away some of the moisture. "You don't get to cry and make me the bad guy," he murmured.

Shaking her head, she dabbed at her eyes with her napkin. He was right. She knew that tears could be manipulative, so why couldn't she stop? And where was all this emotion coming from?

"Excuse me." Pushing her chair back, she stood and walked to the ladies' room. There she cried some more, cursing at herself the entire time. Reed was never going to forgive her, but it wasn't as if he was the last man on earth. She rationalized her behavior with thoughts of being tired and stressed with their work on the task force. In all honesty, working closely with him had shown her sides of him that hadn't surfaced during their dates. Marina washed her face and fixed her makeup. If anyone had told her that she would end up crying over Reed Crawford, she wouldn't have believed it.

When she got back to the table, Reed had already paid the bill. The rest of her food had been put in a take-out carton. Opening her purse, she reached for her wallet.

He waved his hand dismissively. "No. I've already taken care of it."

"I should be getting home," she said politely, not bothering to sit. She'd done enough apologizing.

Retrieving her carry-out carton, he stood and they left the restaurant. Back in the car, he twisted in the seat to face her and ask, "Are you okay?"

Reed always cared. That was one of the things she liked most about him. Hearing him verbalize it made her feel that much better.

"Disappointed, but otherwise fine," she answered flippantly. "You're not much for giving people second chances when it comes to your feelings."

Clenching his jaw, he sighed heavily. "How long have I known you? Ten years? You drop the boyfriends, the almost boyfriends, and move on. You don't do reruns."

"Maybe you're different from the rest?" she suggested.

"Oh, I am," he attested. "Thought you knew it, too."

Nodding, she lifted her hands in a helpless gesture. "Okay, I blew it. Forget I said anything."

"Just like that?"

"Just like that," she confirmed. Reaching for the seat belt, she turned to face the front of the car. He was going to drive her crazy.

"You're pouting."

Marina bit down on the inside of her jaw. "No. Don't flatter yourself."

"You're pouting," he insisted, a smirk in his tone.

"If you say so," she retorted, letting her head relax against the headrest and forcing her folded arms into a more relaxed pose. She didn't need to win this childish argument.

She did turn to look at him then and saw that he'd been razzing her. Deep down she knew she deserved it but it didn't make her feel any better. She felt too raw and emotional to discuss it any further. With an effort she pulled in her bottom lip and relaxed her facial muscles.

Back at the station she gathered her things, said good night and headed for her car.

"What are you doing this evening?" Reed asked a bit too casually.

Was he rubbing salt in the wound? she wondered.

She'd wanted to spend it with him. "Probably see a movie with a friend if I'm not too tired," she lied. The evening would be spent working off some of her frustration in the gym. "What about you?"

"I'll probably work off some of the Italian food we ate and then it's my turn to check on Mom."

She gave his face a quick assessment. The faint bruises were nearly gone. They were another source of negative emotion with her. The last thing Reed needed was another run-in with whoever was stalking him. "Going to call for backup?"

"Nah, I can handle it," he said smoothly.

Alone? "Well, have a good evening," she replied, and kept walking. In her head, another battle raged. There'd been no new ambushes, but she had a strong hunch about Reed in the old neighborhood tonight. Was she going to back up a macho man who didn't want any help?

Chapter 14

Marina knew which Xsport Fitness Gym Reed liked to work out in. He was a creature of habit. She even knew his routine, so it was nothing for her to go home, change into workout gear and plan her routine around his so she could work out without being seen. The gym was enormous. She quit early so she could get back to the ancient Honda she'd borrowed from her neighbor so Reed wouldn't recognize her car. If nothing happened, he'd never know she'd followed him, she reasoned as she waited for Reed to leave.

Dusk was falling when Reed finally came out. He walked casually, scanning the area so thoroughly that she scooted down in the seat. Following him brought back memories of her training days at the academy.

Once she was certain that he was traveling to his mother's house, she turned off and took a shortcut.

It was almost dark when she arrived and scoped out the neighborhood while pretending to look for an address. Residents were abandoning their porches for the lighted security of their homes. A majority of the streetlamps were burned out or missing.

She didn't see anyone lurking or hanging around but that meant next to nothing. The neighborhood was run-down. What she was doing was dangerous and she did not have the jurisdiction to be backing up a cop in this situation. She pushed herself with the knowledge that she was helping a friend.

A block away from Trudy's, Marina parked on the side street. Pulling a baseball cap over her hair, she stepped out of the car in loose dark clothing. The alley yawned ahead of her, looking dark and dangerous. A lesser woman alone could have been taking her life in her hands.

Marina didn't know this alley, but she knew stealth. It was high on her list of skills. She listened to the sounds of the night, becoming one with them.

As she employed the masculine stride she'd perfected in classes that focused on creating disguises, comfort came when she thought of her hand-to-hand combat training, fitted her fingers around the trusty Glock pistol in one pocket and touched the cell phone in the other. There was even a pair of handcuffs in her back pocket, left over from an academy class that covered subduing suspects. She could do this and unless

Reed was attacked and overwhelmed, he'd never even know she'd backed him up.

Stepping into the alley, she picked her way carefully, keeping to the cover of bushes and trees. On occasion she used the sides and backs of garages for cover. Once she'd started, the first block's alley breezed by. A third of the way down the alley of Trudy's block, she heard Reed's car. A dark figure up ahead hopped a fence and was followed by another.

Ducking into the bushes, Marina's breath hitched. Peering into the dimness she hoped there were no more than two potential assailants. Maintaining stealth, she sped up, determined to reach Trudy's before anything happened.

The sharp sound of breaking glass fractured the night. Marina hurried, almost running. At Trudy's back gate she hesitated, listening. She heard the muffled sounds of blows followed by masculine grunts. Two shadowy figures were fighting in the dark. Where was the other person?

Covered by the noise accompanying the fight, Marina used her hands to propel herself over the fence and step lightly down onto the sidewalk in the yard. Intent on locating the other possible assailant, she closed on the edge of the garage.

An arm snaked out in the darkness, dragging her forward. Sensing the right fist following it, Marina ducked and used the forward motion to roll. Down, and half on the grass and half on the sidewalk, she kicked out, landing blows to the thighs and a lucky one to her assailant's crouch.

With a high-pitched cry of pain, he bent over, backing up. Adrenaline surging, she scrambled to her feet, punching and kicking.

He went down.

Pressing her advantage, Marina smashed his nose with her fist. While he writhed in pain she rolled him over and secured his wrists with the cuffs from her back pocket.

With her attacker immobilized, Marina spared a glance for Reed and his beefy assailant. They were on the grass, punching each other in a battle worthy of a heavyweight championship bout. With a savage burst of energy, Reed decimated the other man with the brutal thunder of his fists. Dazed, his assailant fell and cowered behind his outstretched hands. Latching onto one arm, Reed turned and cuffed him in a smooth, effortless motion.

Police sirens sounded in the distance. Marina glanced up to see Trudy's silhouette in the back bedroom window. She must have called the police.

As the sound increased in volume, Marina considered cutting down the alley. Her presence would take a delicate explanation. So damned what, she mused finally. *I haven't done anything but defend myself.*

"Marina? I heard someone else fighting. You okay?" Reed called.

She realized then that her disguise wasn't good enough to fool Reed. "Fine," she answered. "No rush, but I've got someone back here waiting for you."

Reed chuckled. With a knee in his assailant's chest, he fumbled with something in his back pocket. She focused, trying to see it in the dark and failing. He aimed it at his assailant.

Marina released an audible sigh when bright light from Reed's flashlight illuminated the man's face.

Reed gazed at the man in shock. "Anthony!"

"Yeah, Mr. Big Time Police Detective. It's me!"

"Why?" Reed demanded in a harsh tone.

Struggling like a wild bull, he tried to break free. "You can't hold me."

Adjusting his weight and his grasp, Reed held on to him. "Why?" he repeated.

Anthony glared up at him, his eyes full of venom and hatred. "Because we wanted to bring you down and it's personal. We don't like how you caught Chelsie and dragged him out in the street like he wasn't nothing. Chelsie ain't killed nobody."

"If he's innocent, it should come out in court." Reed removed his knee and dragged Anthony to his feet.

"You expect me to believe that shit?" Anthony sneered. "This time you stepping up on Chelsie's back. You'd give your ass for another promotion."

"I'm going to kick yours some more if you don't stop all the BS." Reed practically growled. "I've had enough. Do you think I don't know he was over the local drug factory?"

The sound of a car hurtling to a stop in the street reached them. Car doors slammed.

"Police!" someone yelled. Footsteps echoed on the sidewalk between the houses. Twin flashlight beams illuminated the darkness.

"Police Officer!" Reed yelled back.

"How'd you like that black eye I gave you last time?" Anthony asked, laughing hoarsely.

"You sucker punched me in the dark, coward." Reed's voice roughened.

"Yeah, but you da hotshot cop, Mr. Big Stuff. You supposed to be ready all the time. I always could scrap better than you, anyway."

"Yeah, that's why I've got you cuffed and ready for the lockup," Reed snapped.

Two cops in uniform rounded the side of the house. "Crawford?" one of them called.

"That's me," Reed answered, shining his flashlight on the badge in his hand. He told the two uniformed patrolmen about being attacked in his mother's backyard. Then he handed over his assailant.

"What about this man on the ground? He's been cuffed."

Marina spoke up. "He attacked me, so I had to defend myself. I'm Special Agent Marina Santos." She flashed her ID.

"And what are you doing here, ma'am?" one of them asked.

"Lieutenant Crawford and I are friends and we're working on a task force project together. I was concerned since he got ambushed in the dark a few days ago, so I followed him here," she explained, hoping she didn't make Reed sound like he was totally incompetent.

"You can follow me home anytime," one of the officers said, flashing her a playful smile.

Happy that this was not going to turn into a jurisdictional issue, Marina ignored him.

"Who's your backup, Anthony?" Reed asked, shining the beam of his flashlight on the slender man lying on the ground in a fetal position. "Dooley," he murmured in dawning recognition.

The man turned his face away from the bright light.

"Will you be pressing charges?" one of uniforms asked Reed as he hauled Dooley to his feet.

"Yes, I will," Reed answered, eyeing Anthony and Dooley. "I'll be down to take care of the paperwork in the morning."

Marina stood on Trudy's front porch with Reed and watched the patrolmen put the two men in the back of the cruiser.

Reed tapped her arm. "Unofficial backup, huh?"

Marina opened her arms and pulled him into a fierce hug. "You were being stubborn and I was worried. Anything could have happened."

"I'm okay." He returned the hug, holding her for several precious seconds more. "Anthony had his backup. I'm glad you were mine."

Being in his arms felt so wonderful that she closed her eyes.

"How'd you know it was me?"

"The sounds you make when you fight, the way you move, and the body underneath those sweats… Girl, I'd know you anywhere." Reed slowly dropped his arms.

Marina tore herself away from him.

He unlocked the front door and pushed it open. "Want to come in for a minute?"

"Why not?" She followed him into the brightly lit interior.

Dressed in a sleeveless housedress, Trudy Crawford sat in a chair at her computer. Seeing Marina, she smiled and greeted her. "I saw you out back fighting and I'm proud of you," she said coyly when Marina came and kissed her cheek. "When I saw that man grab you I thought it was all over."

"I had a lot of training," Marina explained modestly. She wasn't superwoman, but she'd worked hard to hone her skills.

"Training's one thing. Execution is another," Trudy said, smiling at Reed's kiss on her cheek. She studied both of them until she was certain they were fine.

Marina scanned Reed, too, noting that this time he had only a few minor scratches. They'd been incredibly lucky.

Trudy was sad to hear that Reed's attackers had been Anthony and Dooley. They'd grown up with Reed in the neighborhood. She explained that Anthony had recently been kicked out of the army and Dooley's family had fallen on hard times.

Listening, Marina thought about Chelsie Hawkins and the things Reed had said about him. She'd read about his arrest for his girlfriend's murder, but she'd had no idea that Reed was involved or that people were still simmering over the incident. Anthony was apparently angry enough to go after Reed, even if some of his anger was due to the abrupt end to his part in the lucrative drug business. Dooley had attacked her, but she liked to think that if she hadn't shown up, he'd have let Anthony and Reed duke it out alone.

"How's the task force coming?" Trudy asked.

Marina explained that they'd narrowed the list of potential victims but the list of suspects for the serial killer was too long. They had a lot of work to do.

"I didn't know that you and Reed were working the task force together until I saw parts of the press conference on television," Trudy confessed.

Marina shot him a surprised glance. She could only hope she'd kept the little pang of hurt out of her expression.

Reed looked defensive. "I didn't want to get her hopes up. She thought we were getting serious," he muttered.

We were until I messed things up. "We're still friends," Marina told Trudy. It didn't begin to describe how she felt about Reed.

"Good. Then you can come on a double date with me, Reed and my friend, Dr. Jay McNeil."

"Dr. Jay McNeil?" Marina parroted.

"Yes, he's a physician at Providence Hospital. I met him through an Internet dating service," Trudy said proudly.

"Internet dating service?"

"Well he's too busy to date the regular way. This way he can talk to people on the Internet and meet the most promising ones in person."

Making a determined effort not to look at Reed, Marina told Trudy she'd love to come along. Reed accepted the situation gracefully, but Marina was painfully aware that he hadn't asked her to join him. She chatted awhile longer then said good night. Reed drove her to her car.

On the way home, she thought about Reed and all the things they'd been through in the past few days. She wouldn't spend any more time thinking about what could have happened tonight. Instead she turned her thoughts to the serial avenger and tried to match suspects with motives in her head. Some of them had alibis for all but one night.

She had a horrible thought it was possible that all the fraternity's victims knew each other. What if they'd all cooperated enough to take turns committing the murders?

Chapter 15

St. Joseph Hospital was a bustling place. Reed and Marina strode past the full emergency waiting room and the crowded lobby to stop at the information desk. An old man in a blue jacket stood behind the desk, directing people to different areas and issuing room passes for people visiting patients. With a smile, he directed Reed and Marina to an office to the left and two corridors down.

The outer room to Elizabeth Hatcher's office was empty. Peering through the little window at the top of the soundproof inner room, they saw her talking to a roomful of women.

The women sat in a circle of chairs. Watching them, Marina wished she could read lips because Hatcher talked to them at length. A number of the women's faces reflected intense emotion. Some hugged one another. Others cried. Hatcher continued, putting herself into her words with emphatic gestures and the play of emotion on her expressive face.

Reed and Marina hovered near the window, not wanting to disturb the flow of what was happening inside the room or to invade the women's privacy.

Gradually the women calmed, their faces reflecting resignation, strength and hope. Marina could only imagine the message they'd been given.

The session ended. Marina and Reed moved to let the women pass. Several of the women waited to hug Hatcher before they left. Some asked questions and took down numbers.

When the room was empty, Hatcher beckoned them in. "You're waiting to see me?" she asked, taking a long drink from a large bottle of water.

Marina nodded. "Yes, I'm Special Agent Marina Santos and this is my associate, Lieutenant Reed Crawford of the Chicago Police Department."

Hatcher's eyes widened fractionally. "Have you got some new information on the men who've made so many victims of the women I counsel?"

"I guess you could say that." Marina dropped down into one of the chairs. "Lieutenant Crawford and I are on a task force trying to stop a serial killer who has been targeting men."

"I really don't think I can help you with that," Hatcher said, taking another sip of water.

"Oh, but I think you can." Reed moved away from the entryway and took a seat. "We've narrowed the list of victims down to a group of young men who attended Merriwhether University and belonged to the Alpha Kappa Epsilon fraternity."

Hatcher looked puzzled. "I haven't worked at Merriwhether in years."

"The victims in question were at the university three and four years ago," Marina explained.

"I see." Hatcher slowly eased back in her chair. "What is it you want to know?"

"I know that you counseled groups from the Women's Campus Crisis Center there, and the Student Advocate Office," Marina said.

Hatcher set her bottle of water on the table. "Yes, that's correct."

"Well, during that time two of the women you counseled attacked and severely injured a male student on campus…"

"Yes, they confronted their rapist with violence," Hatcher explained, her voice growing sharp. "I didn't condone or suggest they do what they did, but it happened and I got blamed for it."

Reed set the record straight. "Didn't one of the women in question get time in prison for what she did?"

Hatcher tensed her jaw. Her fingers curled over the arms of her chair. "Yes, but the university administration blamed me. After that they started trying to get rid of me. They said I was too controversial. Why are you bringing all this up?"

"We know that Aubrey Russell was attacked by two women. One got away and was never identified. Who was that woman?"

Hatcher was silent for several moments. "Why do you want to know?"

Rubbing her nail against the binding on her notebook, Marina explained. "We've been compiling a list of suspects for the serial killer, gathering information about them and their alibis. Whoever this woman is, she's already committed violence in the past against one of the fraternity members. It's possible that she's found a reason to do it again."

Hatcher eyed them suspiciously. "So you're not trying to send her to prison for something she did back then?"

Reed looked impatient. "Our main concern is finding the serial killer. Plus, Audrey's deceased now. It's over."

Marina studied Hatcher, wishing she could read her mind. "Who was the other woman?"

Hatcher frowned. Her tongue protruded slightly from between her pursed lips. "This could ruin her career," she protested.

"If this woman is not the serial killer, then we can keep this information confidential," Marina confided, trying to get Hatcher to open up.

Still silent, Hatcher bowed her head. Her mouth opened and closed twice.

Marina forced herself to count to ten. She didn't want to resort to threats just yet.

Hatcher's chest rose and fell. Her head came up slowly. She made eye contact with Marina. "It was Sherianne Gellus."

Marina expelled a hard breath. She'd thought Sherianne Gellus was too smart to do something like this. "Aubrey assaulted her?"

Hatcher grabbed the water and took a long desperate-looking drink. "Actually, she managed to get away from that party," she explained. "Her sister wouldn't leave and Sherianne wasn't in any shape to make her."

"We've already talked to Sherianne and we're checking her alibis," Reed said.

"Then this information doesn't have to go any further than this?"

"It won't," Marina assured her, "unless her alibis don't check out."

Hatcher's fingers eased on the arms of the chair. "Is there anything else you want to know?"

Marina set her notebook in her lap. "Yes. Did you keep records on your support groups at Merriwhether?"

"No more than what was required for the university to keep its federal funding. Privacy is a big issue," Hatcher stated flatly. "Whatever I had was turned over to the university administration."

Reed shifted restlessly. "Can you be more explicit? Did you get names? Did you have addresses and phone numbers?"

Hatcher leveled a challenging stare at him. "The women had to give names, but they didn't have to be the right ones. They had to prove that they were students at the university, but we didn't record anything. The names that we knew for certain were those associated with the Student Advocate Office and the court cases."

"I see." Reed let his shoulders drop. "I believe we've already seen those records."

Marina nodded. "That's correct." She faced Dr. Hatcher once more. "Do you remember anyone who really stood out in the groups, someone who might still be angry enough to kill?"

For the first time Elizabeth Hatcher paused dramatically and almost smiled. It looked more like a grimace. "You're already checking the alibis for Sherianne Gellus, and Carrie Ann is dead."

The room got quiet. Marina actually shivered at the sound and content of Hatcher's words. The woman had all but pointed a finger at Sherianne Gellus as the serial killer. Ending the interview, Reed and Marina left in a rush.

Back at the office Marina's first priority was to verify Sherianne's alibis. Tension and excitement ruled her as she checked the statement and spoke with airline and hotel staff.

It was difficult for anyone to remember specifics, given the time that had passed since the first murder, but airline and hotel records supported Sherianne's statement that she'd been in New York when Colton Edwards was murdered. One of her co-workers even saw her let someone on their client's staff into her room late that night.

Sherianne's boyfriend Wyatt's statement effectively covered the night that Elliot had been murdered. He could not recall anything specific for the October date when Aubrey had been murdered. A confidential check of the firm's records revealed that Sherianne had actually been working on a case at the office all night when Aubrey had been killed.

By the end of the day Marina was dragging and ninety-eight percent certain that Sherianne was *not* their serial killer. Shoulders slumped, she sat at her desk, morosely studying the other people on the list.

"I've just cleared Lissa Rawlins, too," Reed informed her. "Have we got any suspects left?"

Marina drummed her fingers on the desk. "Just Jasmine O'Leary, and I think she's going to check out. Maybe we've been going about this all wrong."

"Now don't you start echoing the media on this," Reed warned in a testy voice.

Glancing up, she made eye contact with him. His were a little red and had dark circles underneath. He looked exhausted. They hadn't gotten much sleep lately. "Sorry," she mumbled, "I was just thinking that maybe we should be looking for people who couldn't get into the fraternity or maybe guys who were jealous of the victims."

"No." Reed raked a hand through his hair. "I like the other idea. Lissa killed blank. Sherianne killed blank. Jasmine killed blank."

Marina sighed. "We can't prove that Lissa knew any of the other women. She didn't go to Merriwhether and she's only been in Chicago for a few years. I just told you that I've all but cleared Sherianne. We must be overlooking something."

Reed shrugged. "Well something had better break soon. We're being pulled in to help provide protection for Gerry so we're going to lose task force time. If the serial avenger is someone we haven't thought of, someone close to all of them, then our protection will be a joke. I'm not losing another one of them to this killer."

"Me, either," she replied, racking her brain for ideas. She and Reed had been working hard to solve the case. A fresh perspective would probably show them some things they hadn't thought of. Her fists clenched. Much as she hated the prospect, it was getting to the point where she would have to go to Lowell Talbot for help. The man was brilliant, but she and Reed were good, too. Marina pitted her own professional pride and feelings of competence against the knowledge and experience behind Talbot's brilliance. If someone else died before she and Reed caught the killer, could she live with herself? *One more day,* she promised herself. If they didn't find the killer or more leads, she'd go see Talbot.

Chapter 16

Seated at a table in his favorite restaurant, Gerry Chandler ate his sandwich and tried to pretend he didn't see the undercover cop watching him from two tables over. The surveillance was for his protection and he appreciated it, but after a week he was tired of being watched. Privacy was a thing of the past. In addition he hated having to call the surveillance team whenever he was ready to leave work so that they could tail him. He almost wished the serial killer would make a move on him and get it over with. Almost.

He checked his watch. He needed to leave in the next ten minutes to make it back to work on time. With the cops tailing and watching him, even his work as an environmental analyst was difficult these days. His co-workers who knew he'd gone to Merriwhether had also noticed the increased activity around him that often featured cops in uniform, and put two and two together.

His associates had asked a number of questions he couldn't answer due to task force requests, and the gossip was ridiculous. His boss, Mona, knew the details. Who knew that a few college frat parties with some stupid chicks would lead to threats to his life? Grinding his teeth in irritation, he signaled the waitress for a carry-out bag.

Walking to his car he tried to lift his spirits with the only bright spot in his week. The pay at GTC was okay, but he knew he deserved better. In an effort to see how much he was worth, he'd submitted his résumé to a number of companies and some headhunters. Now he had an interview tomorrow with a brand-new company, Federated Environmental Development—FED—and his prospects looked good. For once he would be able to get in on the ground floor of something and maybe snag a critical role.

Opening his car door, he smiled. He didn't plan on telling Federated Environmental Development anything about there being a serial killer and needing law-enforcement protection so tight that they followed him into the restaurant bathroom. He just wished they'd hurry up and find the crazy bitch that had already killed four men.

Gerry turned the key in the ignition and let his gaze sweep the area. People were going about their business, but he still recognized a few undercover law-enforcement people. As long as he stayed away from women for a while and under task force protection he was safe. Taking off, he assured himself that he didn't have a thing to worry about.

In an unmarked C.P.D. vehicle Reed and Marina drove to Gerry Chandler's apartment. As Reed had predicted, new mayoral and police department initiatives made it necessary for them to become a part of the surveillance team on Gerry Chandler. For the day, their assignment was to tail Chandler, who had a job interview and half a day of work scheduled. Once Chandler completed his interview they'd tail him to work and be free to chase leads until he got off work.

"I've never heard of Federated Environmental Development," Marina remarked from the passenger seat.

Reed shot her a quick glance. "You mean, you haven't seen it on the financial pages of the newspaper?"

"No and I couldn't find them on the Internet, either."

"It is a new company startup. It may be a while before they show up on the financial pages, looking for investors," he reasoned. "Maybe they're not as far along as they want Chandler to think."

"That would be my guess." Marina resumed looking out the passenger window.

Three doors down from Chandler's condo, Marina called to let him know they'd arrived. Minutes later Chandler hurried out of his upscale condo. His black power suit provided a nice contrast to his red hair and green eyes.

They tailed him to a tall building downtown and watched him enter. Since it was unfamiliar territory, Reed got out and followed Chandler into the building while Marina stayed in the car watching the entrances. He even managed to get on the polished-brass-accented elevator with Chandler and several other people.

On the sixteenth floor, Reed and Chandler were the only people to get off. The halls were deserted except for a few workmen setting up equipment and a few others seen painting in one of the offices. Reed knew that the entire floor was being remodeled for its new tenants, but he'd expected to see a few businesspeople. After all, the workmen could not remodel all the offices at the same time. Of course it was only about eight in the morning and businesses usually opened at nine or ten.

Reed stayed a third of the hall behind Gerry until the man entered a suite with the temporary FED logo sign on the door. Something about the scene niggled at his consciousness, but he couldn't figure it out. He noted that most of the permanent office signs and logos had been removed. Strolling past the office, he was sorry that he'd promised Gerry he wouldn't actually come in. He satisfied himself with the businesslike sounds of the conversation that reached him from the outside of the door.

Riding the elevator down, he decided to find the building's coffee shop and to get coffee and breakfast sandwiches. He made a quick call to Marina to let her know, then found the coffee shop at the end of a confusing set of corridors.

* * *

Gerry sat on the couch in the empty outer office and tried to appear confident. FED's office secretary wasn't even in yet. He'd been on time, but his interviewer, a Ms. Lockwood, apparently wasn't prepared. She'd come out of her office briefly, introduced herself, and offered him coffee.

Coffee made him antsy, but he'd still been nervous enough to drink half a cup. Now his stomach roiled. He hoped he wasn't going to be sick. That would be a quick way to kill the interview and any chance he had of getting the job. He wished he'd taken the time to eat something. When his stomach moaned loudly he swallowed the rest of his coffee, hoping that would shut it up.

Ms. Lockwood's office door opened and she motioned him in. The furniture wasn't as nice as he'd been expecting, but he knew that the entire floor was going through a remodeling process and FED was only using the office in its present condition to interview potential staff members.

He couldn't get over the feeling that he'd seen Ms. Lockwood somewhere before. Her dark hair and deep brown eyes would have been mousy on many women, but Ms. Lockwood was stunning. The body beneath her navy-blue suit was first-class, too. If this wasn't the middle of a job interview and if he hadn't sworn off women until the serial killer was caught, he'd be putting the moves on her.

She motioned him to a seat in the leather guest chair.

"I can't tell you how impressed we are with your résumé," she said, settling into her own chair. "Give me some of the details of your assignments at GTC."

Gerry wasn't feeling very well. Nausea threatened to pull him from his chair and Ms. Lockwood sounded like she was speaking from the other end of a tunnel. He took a minute to collect his thoughts then told her about the analysis he'd done on the impact a proposed new subdivision would have on the water table, the assignment he had to make recommendations for the location for a new incineration center for the city, and the job he'd had consulting and helping Pellaco with a toxic waste cleanup.

Ms. Lockwood nodded encouragingly. "Any other projects?"

Waiting while someone in the kitchen made the breakfast sandwiches, Reed stood at the counter with the coffee he'd fixed for Marina and himself.

"New in the building or just visiting?" the gray-haired old man behind the counter in tired black pants and a worn white shirt asked pleasantly.

"Just visiting." Reed smiled and prepared to make idle conversation. "I had to drop a friend off for a job interview and I'm waiting for him to finish."

"Really? Which company?"

Reed thought twice before answering and revealing the company name but then he reasoned that a startup company would likely have several interviews going on. Giving the information wouldn't necessarily highlight

Gerry Chandler and put him in danger. "Federal Environmental Development, FED."

The old man cocked his head to one side. "I never heard of them."

Reed shrugged. "Me, either, but they're a new company starting up in this building on the sixteenth floor."

"We've got a lot of new businesses coming in since they started fixing up the place," the old man said proudly. "Where's the interview?"

Given their conversation, that was an odd question. "The sixteenth floor," Reed answered, looking puzzled.

"The sixteenth floor?" The old man's gray brows went up and he shot Reed an incredulous look. "I don't think so! All the offices on that floor have been closed due to the remodeling. The building management didn't want to take a chance on someone getting hurt and causing their insurance to go up."

It was Reed's turn to look surprised. His mind raced toward the inevitable conclusion. "No. Maybe they're doing the interviews while other offices are being remodeled. I went up there with him, saw him go into the office, and heard him talking to someone. Are you sure all the offices on the sixteenth floor are closed?"

"I've got it here in black and white." He showed Reed a memo that had been sent to the building's occupants. Reed scanned it quickly.

To Whom It May Concern:
By order of the management, all offices on the

building's sixteenth floor will be closed for
remodeling until further notice. We cannot be
responsible for injury or damage to people, equipment, and furniture in the area while the remodeling effort proceeds, so please govern yourselves
accordingly.

Sincerely,

The Management

The sheet of paper slid from Reed's fingers and
floated on the air as he shoved a hand into his pocket.
Pulling out a crumpled twenty, he slammed it on the
counter. "This is for the breakfast sandwiches and
coffee, but I'm going to have to come back and get
change later."

"Sure. Somebody running a scam on your friend?"
the old man called as Reed shot out of the coffee shop.

Reed was already sprinting down the hall. He wished
that whatever was happening to Gerry Chandler was as
simple as a scam. He could only hope he'd make it in
time to save Gerry's life.

Running up another corridor he missed a turn and
had to double back. He was out of breath when he
reached the elevators. There was no one waiting. He
called Marina and quickly gave her the facts. Then he
called for backup.

Reed gave the elevators another impatient glare. They
hadn't moved much while he'd been waiting. Deciding
that he couldn't afford to wait, he ran for the stairs exit.

* * *

Gerry sat slumped in the guest chair. He felt strange. His vision had doubled. A wave of nausea hit him. His last string of words had come out slurred. "I—I'm sick," he muttered plaintively. The words that came out of his mouth bore no resemblance to those he'd formed in his mind.

"Not feeling well?" Ms. Lockwood asked, the sympathetic words not matching her tone of voice or the hardness in her eyes.

Gerry nodded, abruptly realizing that he was in trouble.

She opened the desk drawer and pulled out a wicked-looking knife with serrated edges.

Gerry tried to push back in his chair and get up, but couldn't find the strength.

"You don't remember me, but I *remember* you. I was one of the women caught in your sick little game. Didn't you ever wonder how the women felt when you put that stuff in their drinks? *Now you know.*" She traced a blood-red manicured nail down the length of the knife. "I'm going to take *good* care of you Gerry. You won't be able to move or call out, but you'll be alert enough to feel everything I'm going to do to you."

Standing, she walked around the edge of the desk to where he sat. "Don't bother to get up." She laughed.

Gerry whimpered as she spun his chair around and closed in, knife extended.

Chest burning, Reed reached the top of the steps for the sixteenth floor. He turned the knob and pulled open the door. Running past workmen busy removing fixtures near the stairs he headed to the suite where he'd left Gerry.

He drew his gun and gently turned the knob. He carefully eased open the door. The outer office was empty except for a secretary's desk and a couple of chairs. Reed stepped inside and closed the door.

He took a moment to acclimate himself and to listen for voices. The low murmur of someone talking pulled him in the direction of the first office. A woman was grunting. Reed paused. The sounds could have been those of someone having sex. Or someone stabbing another person, he decided, regrouping.

Reed pulled open the door. A dark-haired woman in a blue suit bent over Gerry with a bloody knife. Gerry's eyes were open and unmoving. He appeared dazed or dead. Not dead, Reed amended. He saw the faint rise and fall of Gerry's chest. Gerry's blood covered the woman's hands, his shirt, open pants and the leather chair.

Knife raised, the woman turned to face Reed with startled brown eyes.

"Put the knife down and move away from him," Reed ordered, pointing his gun at her.

The woman hesitated. She stared down at the blade and back at Gerry.

Planting his feet, Reed tightened his finger on the trigger. "I'm going to tell you one more time, then I'm going to start shooting."

"I'm the victim here." The woman vented angrily. "He's got to get what's coming to him!"

Reed didn't argue with her. He knew that she could still plunge the knife into Gerry's chest and kill him. He prepared to shoot the knife out of her hand.

Shaking, the woman suddenly dropped the knife and backed away. She crouched against the opposite wall, crying.

He heard the sounds of the construction activity in the hall grow louder as the outer door opened and closed. He caught Marina's scent in the air.

"It's Marina, Reed," she called. Then she was right behind him, filling the doorway. "I've got her covered if you want to see what you can do for Gerry."

Nodding, Reed put his gun away and hurried over to Gerry. He checked the man's neck for a pulse. It was still there, but weak. Several slashes and puncture wounds marred his chest and abdomen. Using Gerry's shirt and jacket, he tried to stem the flow of blood. It was an impossible task. The man needed the skills of a surgeon. "Did you call for an ambulance?" he asked Marina.

"Yes, they should be here in the next ten minutes."

Not really focusing on Reed's face, Gerry talked. Reed couldn't understand any of it. He seized the moment to Mirandize the woman huddled against the wall. Then asked, "What did you give him?"

Marina moved closer to her, repeating the question in a calm, no-nonsense tone.

The woman lifted her head, wiping away tears with her forearms. "Rohypnol. It's what he gave me."

Recognizing the name of one of the drugs used in date

rape, Reed studied Gerry. The drug had incapacitated him and made it easy for this woman to nearly kill him.

"The drug should wear off in eight to twelve hours," Marina said. "I'm more worried about those wounds. We're lucky he hasn't gone into shock."

"He's lucky," Reed countered. "A few more minutes and she would have finished him off."

Marina focused on the woman. "What's your name?"

It took two tries to get an answer. Easing down until she was sitting on the floor, the woman raised her head and met Marina's gaze with a mixture of fear and defiance. "Sandra Nichols."

Checking for Gerry's pulse once more, Reed thought the name sounded familiar. He saw a nearly imperceptible spark of recognition in Marina's eyes, too. His best guess was that Sandra was on the list of the fraternity's victims.

The outer door slammed open. "Police!" a breathless voice barked.

"We're in the first office," Reed yelled. "We have a stabbing victim and his attacker."

Uniformed cops crowded into the room. Reed and Marina identified themselves.

Reed pointed to the woman who was now wringing her bloody hands. "When I opened the door to this office, she was hovering over him with that knife. I nearly had to shoot her to make her put it down. She says her name is Sandra Nichols. The victim is Gerry Chandler."

Surrounding the woman, the officers handcuffed her.

"You two will have to come down to the station to file your report," one of the officers said.

"We'll be filing our report at the Twenty-fourth District Town Hall Station on Halstead. That's where the task force office is located," Reed said.

"Just make sure you do," another officer instructed.

"Where is that ambulance?" Marina asked, casting Gerry a worried look.

He wasn't moving and the amount of blood he'd lost seemed like more than anyone could lose and still live.

"They were waiting at the elevator with a stretcher when we ran up the stairs," one of the officers explained. "This building is old and the elevators are slow. They couldn't have made it up sixteen flights of steps with a stretcher."

"Well we've got to get moving," another officer said as he hustled Sandra toward the door.

The other produced a plastic bag and used an ink pen to maneuver the bloody knife into it. Then both officers left with their prisoner.

Hearing the outer door open once more, Reed called out their location and looked for the Emergency Medical Technicians. Two men hurried in with a stretcher and a couple of med packs. Reed and Marina moved out of the way and let them get to work.

"Will he live?" Marina asked as the EMTs loaded Gerry onto a stretcher.

The taller man spoke with the voice of experience.

"Probably, but from what we can determine, he's in serious condition. We're taking him to Mercy Hospital."

With the uniformed police and Gerry's attacker already gone, Reed and Marina followed the EMTs out of the building.

They watched as Gerry was loaded into the ambulance and hooked up to their equipment. As the ambulance took off with its sirens blaring, Reed turned to face Marina and said, "I think we just caught our serial killer."

Chapter 17

Good news traveled fast. The station was in an uproar with lots of congratulations for the task force. Spaulding had called to personally congratulate Marina, and Reed's spirits were still high from his meeting with Captain Shepherd. They'd wanted to schedule a press conference, but Marina begged for time to check all the paperwork to make sure they hadn't missed anything.

The pressure to perform and to produce was gone now that she'd demonstrated that she could get the job done without having Talbot supervise her every move. But now Marina felt a self-inflicted pressure or need to prove that they had caught the right killer. Sandra had tried to kill Gerry with a similar knife and in a manner similar to the other victims, but had she the motive and opportunity to kill the others? Marina wasn't certain.

Seated at her desk, Marina paged through her files. Sandy Nichols' name appeared in a couple of places. She had been in one of the Merriwhether Campus Crisis Support groups and in one sponsored by the Student Advocate Office. They hadn't been looking for her since they'd cornered Elizabeth Hatcher who gave them Sherianne Gellus as the woman who had helped in the attack on Aubrey Russell years ago.

Marina felt that Hatcher had to have remembered Sandra Nichols. That fact made Marina wonder if the woman had deliberately lied.

She felt Reed's gaze on her. They hadn't said or done anything on a personal level in days, but she would always be sensitive to his moods and thoughts. She'd been trying to keep her thoughts and feelings for Reed out of the work needed to support the case against Sandra Nichols and the closing down of the task force.

Marina glanced up. There was a question in Reed's eyes.

"What? What is it? What are you looking for?" he asked.

She shrugged. "I'm not sure. It's just that this was too easy."

Reed's breath came out in a huff. "I don't call all the work we've done easy. We've been busting our asses on this one," Reed countered. "We even caught her in the act. What more could you want?"

"I want to know why she killed all the others and I want to be sure she could actually have done it. I want to be sure no one helped her. Most of all, I want to be sure that none of the others is going to die because of the nasty crap they did in that fraternity."

"I've been checking the files, too," Reed admitted. "There's no issue as far as motive and opportunity with the murder of Aubrey Russell. He's one of the men accused of assaulting her. Other than the fact that Elliot and Colton were in the fraternity and were accused of doing the same thing to other women, there's no connection."

"Let's go back over her statement to the police," Marina suggested. "I was tired when I read through it the first time, but something about it doesn't quite click. I've been meaning to read it again."

Sipping large cups of coffee, Reed and Marina went through Sandra's statement line by line. Near the end Sandra had been asked to account for her whereabouts on the nights that Aubrey Russell, Colton Edwards and Elliot Washington had been killed. She'd had outpatient surgery on the night Elliot had been killed. It was highly unlikely that she'd killed Elliot Washington.

"Highly unlikely, but not impossible," Reed murmured. "I'll check with SaintCloud to see if what they found at the building matches with what they found with the other victims."

While Reed made the call, Marina paced, trying to ignore the unsettled feeling in the pit of her stomach. Resources had been pulled away from protecting the serial killer's potential victims but she'd talked to them and asked them to lay low and be careful until the task force was certain that the serial killer had been caught. She heard an urgent note creep into Reed's tone.

"What? Are you sure?"

Turning, she came close and tried to listen.

"Anything else?" Bracing, Reed looked as if someone had thrown a glass of water in his face. He grew more intense by the second.

Marina stood close, clenching and unclenching her fists and only catching tantalizing bits of the conversation.

Reed finished and hung up the phone. "The knife Sandra used isn't the same type as the knife used by the serial killer and the wounds themselves are different. Sandra jabbed Gerry with the knife in the stomach and abdomen. The serial killer jabbed and pulled the knife through the organs of the other victims…"

"Shit!" Marina bit her lip. She'd known something wasn't right with Sandra as the serial killer. "Who's the next victim?"

"Harrison Hicks," Reed bit out.

Marina called Hicks' office and discovered that he'd taken some time off.

"We'd better get over there." Marina pulled open a drawer and retrieved her purse.

Reed grabbed his keys. "At least we didn't announce that the serial killer had been caught. Of course by now, the real serial killer would have noticed that the surveillance had been dropped on the potential victims."

The ride to Harrison's home was short and tense. They'd called on the way and gotten no answer. The neat house was locked and Harrison's car was gone. Another call, this time to the surveillance team, and they discovered that Harrison had planned a trip to his cabin near the Blackwell Forest Preserve near Collins, Illinois. He'd even talked John Stuart, the next potential victim, into coming along.

Reed jotted down the address and the directions. It was a five-and-a-half-hour drive. They tried dialing the cabin phone number, but it seemed to be out of order. Neither Hicks nor Stuart was answering their cell phones.

"I don't like the way this is turning out," Marina confided as they turned the car toward the Blackwell Forest Preserve. "If the serial killer has been watching them, she can easily knock them both off without any witnesses."

"Hey, our careers aren't in the toilet yet," Reed admonished. "We could always alert the local police, but we're not sure that anything's wrong."

Trying to get herself to relax, Marina agreed. "Let's just go and see for ourselves. I don't mind using some of my personal time or getting stuck for tonight. We could drive back in the morning. After almost losing Gerry, I'm not sure our luck's going to hold."

Reed gave her the look. "It's not luck. It's investigative analysis, skill and timing. We make a good team, Marina."

She let herself smile at that. "Yes, we do."

Reed insisted on doing all the driving. They stopped

only to use the public bathrooms and to pick up the fast-food they ate on the road.

It was getting dark when Reed turned the car up a trail and arrived at the cabin. The lights were on inside, but no one sat on the porch swing behind the screens.

"How do you want to play this?" Marina asked, noting that Reed had parked the car behind a line of trees just out of sight of the cabin.

He checked his gun. "I'll go first."

"We're a team," she reminded him.

"Yes, but I think it's better if the people in the cabin think I'm alone, at least until we're sure everything's okay. We don't need to present two threats right off."

Marina put a hand on his arm. "Let me go first. Women are less threatening, especially to another woman."

Reed tossed her an impatient look. "I'm a cop, Marina. This is what we do."

"I'm an FBI agent. This is my case, too," she replied stubbornly.

They stood at an impasse for several seconds.

"Marina," he intoned in that deep voice, dragging out the syllables.

Against her better judgment, Marina relented. "Okay, if you insist, but next time you give in."

He didn't add a comeback, but his lips twisted with amusement. She knew that he was not going to give in easily. Biting her lip, Marina wanted to kiss him, to wish him luck, but that would only clue him in to the fact that she was afraid for him.

Reed opened the driver's door and got out. "Stay here. If I'm not back in fifteen minutes, come and get me."

With fear for Reed eating at her, she watched him check out the front and back of the cabin.

Unable to stand the suspense any longer, she got out of the car and edged closer to the structure.

Reed stood in front of the cabin, knocking on the door. He froze momentarily, and she knew he'd become aware that she was close.

A tall, attractive blonde in a dark tunic and slacks with gold sandals answered the door. Her true features were hard to discern beneath the thick layers of a perfect makeup job, but enough remained to tease Marina's memory. Marina studied her, wondering where she'd seen her before.

In the background, Marina saw John Stuart sitting at a table inside. Where was Harrison Hicks? Marina stared at the blonde, wondering if she could be their serial killer. If so, she could have already killed Harrison.

Reed and the blonde exchanged words. Marina couldn't hear what they said, but she could see almost everything. Suddenly they were struggling over something. Focusing, she saw that it was a gun. Two shots rang out. One went wild. The other happened when the gun was so close that it had to have hit one of them.

Marina's heart pumped double-time. Who shot who? Studying them, she prayed for Reed to be all right.

Both Reed and the woman were still standing. Marina drew her gun and edged closer, weighing options.

Fear for Reed crawled up from her belly and crowded her throat. Her angle on Reed and the woman changed and she saw that both were still holding on to the gun. Even worse, Marina didn't have a clear shot.

Marina struggled to breathe. She realized that she'd been holding her breath. Her only comfort was the fact that Reed was still conscious and talking.

She had to do something to save Reed. Marina brought the pistol up.

Reed stumbled and went down.

The impact slammed into Marina with the force of a category five hurricane. *Dear God, am I going to lose Reed forever?* Marina squeezed off a shot.

The bullet scorched a path through the woman's hair. With a yelp, she jumped.

"Move away from him," Marina ordered in a tone laced with steel.

The woman complied, easing behind the cover of the cabin door. As Marina edged closer, the woman pushed it closed.

Dear God! Marina sprinted forward and leaped onto the porch. Crouching, she leaned over Reed. His eyes were open. "I'm okay," he told her.

"No, you're not," she snapped, tears burning her eyelids. There was a rapidly spreading red stain near the bottom of his shirt. "Is that a stomach wound?"

"Below that," he rasped. "Intestines, I think, and it hurts like hell."

"Can you shoot if I put the gun in your hands?"

"Sure, but I won't be moving too fast."

Drawing his gun, Marina put it into his hands. "I've got to try to save Harrison and John."

Reed nodded.

Marina turned and shot out one of the tires on the blue Ford parked in the yard. Then she pushed the cabin door open.

A door opened and running footsteps echoed in the back of the cabin.

Keeping to cover as much as possible, she made it to the table. John sat in a chair facing sideways, glassy-eyed and unmoving. He'd been drugged, but was otherwise not hurt. Harrison was nowhere in sight. She didn't have time to look for him now.

A shot echoed from the porch.

Reed! Did she finish him off? Marina came running.

He was lying on the porch with a big grin. "I think I winged her." He pointed to one of the trails. "She went running that way."

Marina maneuvered herself to the edge of the porch and dropped down behind the safety of a bush. "I'm going after her. John's inside drugged, but I can't find Harrison."

"Get going. I'll hold up this end," Reed said. "I'll call for help."

"You sure?" Marina asked, hating to leave him vulnerable and half afraid he might not be alive when she got back.

"Woman, do your job and quit worrying about me. It ain't my time yet."

She pressed her mouth to Reed's and kissed him deep and hard. He tasted like the first time. He tasted like forever. "I love you," she added solemnly as she ended the kiss, just in case she never got the chance to say it again.

"I know," he answered almost smugly, then added, "I fought it, but I never stopped loving you, Marina. Now go."

She took off, not letting herself enjoy the sweetness of the moment. In the darkness of the trail ahead she saw movement. Marina headed straight for it, the promise of love strengthening her.

As she walked deeper along the trail, she was grateful for the sensible walking shoes she'd worn for work. The path was twisted and everything from jutting tree roots to cut stones, rocks, plants and gravel formed obstacles on the path. Marina's steps were nimble and sure from hours spent running and hiking. She resisted the urge to use her flashlight. That would make a target.

Every now and then she paused and listened to the sounds of the night and the sounds of the blond woman making her way down the path. Since she wasn't familiar with the area, she didn't know how long she would be on the path. She sensed that this could go on for miles.

Marina imagined her up ahead, keeping all that blond hair away from tree branches and bushes, scratching the skin left bare by her gold sandals on rocks and gravel. The noises up ahead stopped.

Marina stopped, too. Then she continued silently on all the grass she could find. Something hard smashed into the tree behind her. With a gasp she dropped down to her knees. The blonde had figured out her position and was shooting at her.

Bringing up her own pistol, Marina aimed and fired a couple of shots at the spot where she thought the shots had come from. A quickly silenced yelp followed the impact of one of the bullets. She couldn't believe her luck.

Move in and try to take her or wait to make sure she's down? Marina debated silently. Mentally marking the spot of the lucky shot, she inched forward on her hands and knees till she'd reached the relative safety of a new hiding place. She lay quietly for several minutes, listening for the blonde.

Marina was thinking of going to check the woman's body for a pulse when something rustled in the dark. She listened, as the sound continued, becoming harder to hear as seconds ticked by. Then the sound of falling gravel reached her ears. The woman was getting away.

Barreling out of her hiding place, Marina kept so low to the ground that her knees began to ache with the strain. She headed back to the trail, aware that the woman had a head start.

Up ahead, more gravel fell as the woman ran down the trail. Marina followed through dense foliage. She couldn't see much, so she used instinct, touch and sound.

Realizing that she no longer heard the sounds of someone else on the trail, Marina froze. Something hot zipped by her face and slammed into the tree next to her.

Marina hit the ground next to the trail. Tired of this

cat-and-mouse game, she brought the pistol up once more. When she saw a bit of yellow up ahead she didn't hesitate. She fired twice.

Checking the area for movement and sound, it took a while to get to where she'd seen, aimed and discharged her gun. She found nothing but bushes, rocks, trees and grass. Frustrated, Marina went back to shadowing the edges of the trail.

The chase continued for several minutes. Despite being in shape from time in the gym and aerobic exercises, Marina's knees and chest burned. The trail rose and wound, inclined and fell. The woman fired at her and she fired back.

Peering into the darkness, Marina wasn't sure what she saw. Had she shot the blonde? An owl hooted in the dark, the eerie sound filling the relative silence. And there was another almost imperceptible sound behind the noise the owl made. She strained her ears.

Realization dawned on Marina. The blonde was using the noise the owl made to make her escape. She hurried down the path.

Marina aimed the pistol at the woman revealed through sketchy patches of moonlight, through the trees and bushes. She tried to fire and her weapon merely clicked. She was out of bullets. Stowing the weapon in its holster she focused on finding another way to get the blonde.

Around a bend she saw lights filtering through the foliage. They were nearing the end of the trail. Sucking in a breath she sped up, pushing herself and keeping to the edge of the path as much as possible. The woman hadn't fired the gun in a while, but that didn't mean she was out of bullets.

Ahead, the woman made the bend and started the decline toward the lights. Behind her, Marina was desperate. She'd gained on the woman, but not enough. She didn't even want to think of what would happen if this killer got away.

At the end of the trail just below them, a pair of high-beam headlights suddenly switched on. The woman slowed, covering her eyes with one hand.

Marina launched herself from the top of the bend to downward path. She landed on the woman, bringing her down and winding them both.

Twisting on the ground, the woman tried to reach the gun she'd dropped. Marina used her fists, punching her in the back of the head and chin. The woman took it in stride, trying to elbow Marina as she dragged them both toward the gun.

This woman was strong and more muscular than any Marina had ever encountered. She couldn't rid herself of the notion that something wasn't right. She grabbed the woman's hair in an effort to pull her head back. Marina yelped as all the hair came off in her hand. Dropping it, she realized that it was a blond wig.

The woman's hand closed on the gun.

With both fists Marina pounded the back of the woman's head, smashing her face into the gravel. The woman grunted, then moaned in pain. Still her fingers curved around the grip.

Marina pounded the woman's head once more and twisted her other arm behind her back with all the force she could muster. The gun went off. The bullet traveled away from them.

Maintaining her position on the woman's back, Marina applied pressure to the woman's well-toned arm, pushing the elbow upward. She heard the gun click. It was empty.

The woman dropped the gun.

Using techniques she'd learned at the academy, Marina caught the woman's wrist and forced her to her feet.

The woman's face was cut and bleeding. The thick makeup had smeared, giving her face a cartoon masklike appearance. She seemed dazed. Both women were still breathing hard. Marina made an effort to focus on keeping the woman secured and getting her into custody.

It was hard not to stare at the face. She knew this person. The secret of the woman's identity hovered, just out of reach. Marina ground her teeth in frustration.

The high beams at the end of the trail switched to regular. Marina recognized Reed's unmarked car. As she approached with her prisoner, the passenger door opened and he eased out. There was a lopsided grin on his face. "Good catch," he muttered.

She focused on his face. "Where's John?" she asked, accepting the pair of handcuffs he offered and placing them on the woman's wrists.

"He's in the back," Reed answered proudly.

Marina quickly glanced at Reed. He was actually on his feet. How had he managed that? John had been drugged and was most likely unconscious and Reed had been hurt enough to stay prone on the cabin porch.

"I couldn't leave you out here with no backup," Reed confessed.

She didn't want to think of what it may have cost him. Her gaze fell to his shirt. The bottom was soaked with blood. Pure grit and determination had pulled him through it. She caught her breath. "You need an ambulance."

"It's coming," he assured her. "And I already called the boss and filled him in. He's the one who put the call in to the locals and your boss, too. Here, put our killer in the front seat. I've already taken the key out and there's nothing she can use to get free."

"W-what about you?" she asked, already muscling the woman closer.

"Don't worry about me." Reed slid along the side of the car and left the driver's door open.

Marina shoved the heavy, handcuffed woman onto the seat. The end of her shirt rolled up to reveal something that looked like an old-fashioned corset. It was a corset. None of the women she knew bothered with girdles, let alone corsets.

She gave the woman's curly brown hair another glance and shut the door with an abrupt realization.

The insight that had been flashing in the back of her mind was mind numbingly clear. Shaking her head she glanced in at the figure on the front seat once more, wondering why she hadn't realized it earlier. Maybe female diva impersonator RuPaul's secrets weren't so secret after all. The woman on the seat wasn't any woman. It was Harrison Hicks in drag.

"Did you find Harrison?" Reed asked, easing down the side of the vehicle to sit on the ground.

Stunned, she didn't know how to explain the night's events. Was Harrison their serial killer or had he simply decided to join in by murdering John? The biggest question was, why? Still puzzling over her realization, she told Reed about Harrison.

Reed burst out laughing. "You're kidding."

"See for yourself," she challenged, easing down to the ground beside him.

"I can't get up right now," he said in a voice that was much too calm.

"Where's the nearest hospital? I'm going to drive you there," she declared, desperate to save his life.

Reed caught her hand. "I've already called for an ambulance and backup. They should be here any minute. We can't risk getting lost on the way to the hospital."

"Reed." She grabbed his arm, fear clutching her insides.

"I know, don't die on you."

"Promise me?" she asked, fighting the sting of tears in her eyes once more.

"Yeah. You'd better take this." He pulled the gun from his holster and offered it.

She took it. "Where is that damned ambulance?"

Reed just stared at her. His eyes looked feverish.

Tears slid down her cheeks.

"Stop crying and talk to me," he said roughly.

Gathering him close in her arms, she rubbed her face against his. "You shouldn't waste your strength talking."

"What else is there to do?" he challenged. "Unless you want to jump my bones."

"You're crazy!" Marina pressed her lips to his seeking mouth, savoring his taste, deepening the kiss and filling it with her passion. She knew that he was trying to distract her and it was working.

He kissed her with an urgency that almost made her forget he was a wounded man. Almost.

His lips stopped moving. Despite the warm night his skin felt shockingly cool against hers. She heard the faint sound of an approaching siren. *Please God, let it be the ambulance for Reed.*

Pushing back from their embrace, she glanced down at him. "Reed, I hear the ambulance."

His eyes were closed, his body limp. With her fingers she checked for his pulse. She found it, faint but steady. Reed was unconscious.

Marina fixed her gaze on the main road just visible beyond the line of trees surrounding the parking lot and prayed.

Chapter 18

The two ambulances arrived with a couple of cars full of police officers. Marina flashed her badge and answered questions while the EMTs worked on Reed and John Stuart. Some of the officers remembered seeing her and Reed on the news doing the task force press conference.

As the police loaded Harrison into the back of one of their cruisers, she noticed that Harrison seemed almost catatonic. He hadn't made a sound since she'd fought him on the trail.

"We'll have a psych doctor take a look at him," one of the officers assured her.

Unable to keep her distance, Marina excused herself to watch the emergency crew take care of Reed. Fear gripped her, tightening around her body and draining her strength.

The equipment and monitors in the back of the ambulance beeped and chirped noisily, emphasizing the seriousness of what was happening with Reed. Studying the screens and monitors she knew that as long as they continued working without sounding an alarm, Reed was still alive.

Marina hesitated, torn between going to the hospital with Reed and staying to take care of task force business with the police. If Reed was dying there was no decision to be made. She would be going with him to the hospital, no matter what. She climbed into the back of the ambulance.

"Is he going to make it?" she asked the emergency tech bending over him.

"His condition is serious," the woman replied as she inserted an IV line and adjusted the flow. "But his vital signs have stabilized. Unless there are other complications, he should be able to recover. Of course it's just my opinion. I'm not a doctor," the tech added. She'd already removed his shirt and attached sensors to his chest. Pointing to Reed's wound on his lower torso, the tech remarked, "Bullet wound?"

"Yes," Marina confirmed. "It was a .38."

"Let's hope the damage to his intestines is minimal. We're taking him to Mt. Zion Hospital. It's about half an hour away."

Swallowing hard, Marina took one last look at Reed. He hadn't moved in several minutes.

"Miss, we're about to take off. We've got to get

him to the hospital as soon as possible," the tech said impatiently.

Marina pressed a kiss to Reed's cool lips and backed away. "I'll come as soon as I'm done here." She climbed out of the vehicle.

"Mt. Zion," the tech reminded Marina as she shut the door. Siren blaring, the ambulance raced for the hospital.

The second ambulance crew had already taken off with John.

Marina's thoughts and emotions were with Reed as she watched the ambulance tear out of the lot and speed down the highway. She felt as though a big invisible fist was squeezing the life out of her. With a tight lease on herself, she led one of the officers up the path to retrieve Harrison's gun. Using a bright flashlight, they found it. Carefully lifting it with a pencil, they placed it in a plastic bag. In the area, they also found several spent shell casings.

Back at Harrison's cabin they waited for the forensics team. Marina used the time to make the difficult call to Trudy, to tell her that her son had been hurt and to give directions to the hospital. Once the forensics team arrived, Marina briefed them on what had happened so they would know what to look for. Then she left for the hospital.

The trip to the hospital in Reed's unmarked car was harrowing for Marina. She'd wiped the seat and steering wheel, but Reed's blood was everywhere. Worse yet was the image imprinted on her brain, of him on the stretcher. Was it too late to fulfill all the hopes and dreams she had for herself and Reed?

At the hospital Marina checked in at the desk. Reed was already in surgery. Bloodwork had been done on John Stuart and they were waiting for the results. Marina ended up in a waiting room full of surgery patient family members.

Fingers tight on the arms of her upholstered chair, she stared at the calming blue walls and prayed. The mood in the room was grim. Doctors came through with news at irregular intervals, garnering cries of relief and joy from some family members and tears of pain and sorrow from other. She watched the entryway each time a doctor appeared, fearing what was to come. She was making herself sick.

Marina checked on John Stuart and was informed that his bloodwork showed traces of Rohypnol. Otherwise he was fine and would be released in the morning.

She called Javier to tell him that she was still in Collins and that Reed had been hurt. He offered to come down to sit in the hospital with her.

"Oh, Dad, I don't want you to go to that much trouble. You know Collins is at least a five-hour drive from Chicago and I'll probably start back sometime tomorrow."

Javier sighed dramatically. "Do you think I can't hear how worried and terrified you are? I want to comfort you, to help you through this. *Mija,* you sound stronger going after a serial killer than you do waiting for Reed to get out of surgery."

"Maybe so, but he'll be out of surgery before you get here. The emergency techs said he should make it unless he had complications."

"Then why do you sound so upset, hmm?"

Marina sucked in a calming breath and said, "The truth is that I'm afraid to let myself believe it. I don't want to be disappointed because I—I love him, Dad. I can't stop worrying until it is over."

"So you love him, huh?"

"Yes, I do."

"Gonna marry him?"

"If he asks, yes."

"He will, *mija,* he will. Will you at least call me when he comes out of surgery, no matter what?"

Marina promised. Then she hung up the phone and returned to the waiting room.

Little by little the waiting room emptied as the night wore on. A tall, slim doctor in blue scrubs entered the room and glanced around. His gaze met Marina's. "Ms. Santos?"

"Yes." Nodding, she stood.

"The bullet damaged Mr. Crawford's colon before exiting. We've been able to repair most of the damage but Mr. Crawford was weak from loss of blood. He's in recovery now and doing as well as can be expected. The next few hours will determine where he goes from here. We expect him to make a full recovery. They'll let you see him in about twenty minutes or so."

Grateful for the news, Marina thanked the doctor and left the waiting room. She called Javier with the information. Several minutes later she stood by Reed's bed in the recovery unit and held his hand. He didn't move, but his warmth reassured her. She'd had the scariest night of her life. Determined not to leave until she spoke to Reed, she stayed with him the allowed ten minutes every hour.

Her third time in, he stirred when she took his hand. His eyes opened slowly. It took two tries before his voice came out. "Told you I wasn't ready to check out."

Marina could only smile and grip his hand harder.

"Did you call Ma?"

"Yes, she should be here any minute. Ron is driving her down since there weren't any flights here this time of night."

"I really didn't want to worry her," Reed muttered.

"I had to call her. Ron, too. This was too serious for me to take chances on how things were going to turn out," she countered, thinking about the fear she'd lived through.

Reed's gaze locked with hers. "I wasn't so sure of the outcome, either," he admitted. "My only comfort was the fact that I told you how I felt before things really got bad."

Still holding his hand, she leaned forward and pressed her lips to his. "I don't want to go through anything like this again."

"Me, either, but each day is a gift, so we've got to live life to the fullest," he said. "When I get out of here I'm not holding back on anything."

They exchanged meaningful glances. Marina let herself hope that this time they'd be together for good.

While Reed slept and was finally moved to a room, Marina sat in the waiting room with Trudy and Reed's brother Ron till the wee hours of the morning.

Morning came after a long night, but Marina decided to remain at the hospital long enough to assist the local police in getting John Stuart's statement. It was too good an opportunity to miss.

Sitting up in bed, looking like he was on the wrong end of a drinking binge, John Stuart was glad to be alive. He drained the small pitcher of water by his bed and signaled that he was ready.

"What were you doing at the cabin?" Lieutenant Calvin asked John.

"Harrison offered me a few days to get away from the city since the serial killer had been caught. I took him up on it and we drove down in his car. We had drinks before dinner. Then I started feeling sort of strange. That's when Harrison disappeared into the bedroom and a blond woman came out. It took me a while to realize it was him. I didn't know what to think. I mean, I never knew he was a cross-dresser. Then he started talking crazy, in a woman's voice. It was almost as if he really thought he was a woman, you know?"

"What do you mean, 'talking crazy'?" Marina asked.

"I don't remember exactly what he said. He just gave me a lot of garbage about me not getting away with a crime. He acted like I'd done something to him, like I'd raped him or something. I'm not gay and I've never experimented that way, either."

Pencil poised, she leaned forward. "Then what happened?"

"He took a knife off the table and started playing with it and waving it in my face. I was feeling pretty sick about then. That's when Lieutenant Crawford showed up."

"Why didn't you try to escape?"

"I couldn't move. I think Harrison put something in my drink."

"Rohypnol," Marina said helpfully. "It's a date rape drug."

Glancing down at his sheets for a moment, John turned a little red.

Marina figured it was because this time he'd had a chance to be on the other side of the drug. Hopefully it was enough to keep him from ever using it again.

The lieutenant continued with his questions. "Was there anyone else at the cabin?"

"No." John kept his eyes lowered.

"Did Harrison threaten to kill you?"

"Yes. He was going to use the knife."

The lieutenant held up a photo. "Is this the knife?"

Lifting his eyes to take it in, John blinked, shrinking in on himself. "Yes, that's it. Where's Harrison? He didn't get away, did he?"

"Are you afraid he'll come after you again?"

"Hell, yeah." John swallowed hard. "If Crawford hadn't shown up…"

"We've got Harrison in custody," Lt. Calvin assured him. "Has he threatened anyone else?"

"Not that I know of. I wouldn't have gone to his cabin if he had. He was always a pretty quiet guy. The last guy you'd think of being violent. I remember back when Aubrey was attacked. Harrison was the one who found Aubrey. He was crying and stuttering when he got Aubrey to the hospital. Then he just went into some kind of state and it was a long time before he came out of it."

Marina had seen the file pictures of Aubrey after the brutal beating. Anyone would have been upset, she reasoned, but Harrison could have been unbalanced then. It might help to explain the current situation. She jotted down her thoughts, anxious that she might be grasping at straws.

The pressure was on. If she couldn't prove that Harrison was the serial avenger then he would be charged with attempting to murder Reed and threatening John and holding him against his will. Those charges wouldn't be enough to answer for the deaths so far.

When the interview with John was done, she discussed and compared notes with the lieutenant. They'd both planned to check into Harrison's medical records from his time in college to the present. The lieutenant told her that Harrison had been seen by a doctor and was still in some sort of state. They hadn't been able to get anything out him.

She thought about Harrison, the accusations made about his part in the campus assaults, his cross-dressing to commit a crime, and what he'd done to John Stuart. Somehow they were all connected. Rubbing her forehead with her fingertips, she realized that at the moment it was too much for her frazzled brain to figure out. She was long overdue for sleep.

Reluctantly checking into a local hotel, Marina slept ten hours straight. Afterward she returned to the hospital to see Reed. He looked much better. His color was good and although he nodded off a couple of times, he was coherent and healing. The way he refused to let go of her hand made her feel good.

Marina satisfied herself with being close to him and enjoying the way his eyes lit up when he looked at her.

Trudy simply gave them an indulgent smile. She and Ron had checked in a local hotel and slept for a few hours too. Trudy was hanging on like a trooper, but fatigue was setting in once more. Marina offered to drop her at the hotel before making the drive back to Chicago. Trudy accepted, but insisted on Reed and Marina spending some time alone first.

"Did you get the scoop on Harrison?" Reed asked, tugging her to sit beside him on the bed.

"Not yet, but I will," she promised. "John said Harrison served doctored drinks, went into the bedroom and came out dressed and acting like a crazy woman."

Reed curved an arm around her, pulling her in for an intimate kiss filled with lips and tongue and a passionate desire that was unnerving in a man who had been in surgery for hours the night before. She actually felt a little dizzy.

"I see you're feeling better," she murmured, unable to hold back her smile.

His husky voice filled her ears. "You always make me feel better."

Marina laughed. With a finger she traced a straight path from his forehead to the center of his chest. "Don't start something you can't finish."

"I always finish what I start," he said, giving her the phony version of an injured expression.

She cupped his cheek, reveling in the feel of his razor stubble on her fingers. "I wasn't questioning that. I just hate to get all excited when you're going to be physically limited while you recover," she teased.

This time Reed laughed. "Take me home, Marina. I'll find a way to satisfy you. Guaranteed."

"Stop it, Reed." She pushed at his hands that had slipped from her waist to her hips. "They're not going to let you out of here for at least another day or two."

"So you'll wait for me?"

"I've waited a lot longer than a couple of days for you to come around," she said, suddenly unable to maintain the light, teasing note of their conversation any longer.

"We both messed up," he said, urging her closer, "But we're going to get it right this time, okay?"

"Yes." She leaned down for another kiss. "I've got to get back to Chicago."

"So you'll call me when you get there?"

"Sure." She opened her purse, found a pen and a piece of paper and wrote down the phone number.

"And be careful. Harrison doesn't have to be the killer, you know."

Marina gazed down at him, hating that she had to leave and wishing he'd tell her that he loved her again. She knew that people said a lot when they thought they were dying. Maybe he'd exaggerated his feelings. It wasn't like her to need his reassurance. "Talk to you later," she said, leaving the room to meet Trudy.

Marina took Trudy to the hotel then started the drive to Chicago. She spent most of the trip puzzling over the serial avenger. Was it Harrison? Was he crazy? Never in a million years would she have suspected him, yet they'd caught him. She needed his alibis for the nights of the murders and she needed a motive for the killing.

In the back of her mind she worried that this entire episode would turn out like the one they'd had with Gerry Chandler and Sandra Nichols. Gerry was still recovering at home. Sandra was in jail awaiting trial for her attack on Gerry, but there was nothing else to link her to the murders.

Surely there couldn't be that many past victims waiting to take advantage of the spotlight on the serial avenger to eliminate some of the Alpha Kappa Epsilon members. Shaking her head, Marina drove on.

When she stopped for gas, she called Captain Spaulding and asked that the protection for the men who had been on the serial killer list continue at least until they were certain that Harrison was the serial avenger. He agreed.

Getting back on the road, she couldn't get Harrison Hicks and his glorious disguise off her mind. "Harrison, Harrison," she muttered under her breath, "are you really crazy or are you the best actor we've ever seen?"

Chapter 19

Javier had used his emergency key and was camped out at Marina's house when she arrived home. Getting up from the sofa, he folded her in an emotional hug. "He's okay?" he asked, anxiously studying her face and gleaning something from her demeanor and expression.

"Yes. He'll be back in Chicago in a day or two."

"Good." Javier released her. "I made you some *asopao de pollo*."

"Oh, Dad, thank you!" Marina's stomach whined as she hurried into the kitchen. Food had not been a priority during the past twenty-four hours. Better still, *asopao de pollo* was her favorite comfort food.

She warmed a bowl of the soup in the microwave. Javier sat with her while she ate. Between spoonfuls she smiled at him, sensing that he was waiting for the right moment to tell her something important. "What is it, Dad?" she asked when she could stand it no longer.

"I want to apologize for meddling when you were seeing Reed and Emilio. I should have let you decide between the two."

Marina shook her head vehemently. "It wasn't your fault. I *asked* for your opinion."

"And I should have kept it to myself," he countered. "You love Reed Crawford."

"Yes, but I didn't know it then," she admitted, surprised at how easily this truth flowed from her lips.

"If I hadn't interfered, you might be married now," Javier added soulfully.

Marina laughed. "We'll never know, will we? Don't worry about it, Dad, because Reed and I love each other now."

He nodded. His expression letting her know that he'd accepted her word and her choice, once and for all.

She gave him a speculative glance. "You know, it's kind of hard to see you without a love life."

Javier threw her a mischievous look. "Why don't you introduce me to Reed's mother? She's single, isn't she?"

At a loss for words, Marina's eyes widened. What in the world would she and Reed do if Trudy and Javier actually hit it off?

Javier's resultant laughter said it all. He was just teasing her.

"Just for that, I'm going to set it up," she threatened. Javier just kept laughing.

Tired from the drive and the long night before it, Marina still went in to the office. She was worried that C.P.D. and the FBI might prematurely decide that Harrison was the serial avenger and remove the protection in place for the remaining men on the list.

Determined not to waste any more time, Marina worked with Shepherd and Spaulding to secure a search warrant for Harrison Hicks' home in Chicago. Hours later she led a team of Reed's police buddies and station volunteers in a search of Harrison's home.

Harrison's house was incredibly neat and orderly. The team members wore gloves but there wasn't a speck of dust anywhere. Hidden at the back of his bedroom closet the team found stylish women's clothing and shoes. Several pairs of the heels were taken for comparison to the high-heeled prints found at the site of Alderman Huber's murder.

So Harrison's dressing up like a woman isn't a fluke, Marina mused. Still it failed to explain why he'd tried to kill John.

The team hit the jackpot when they opened a locked file filled with important papers. Under receipts, they found several for visits to a psychiatrist named Dr. Everett Bell.

Marina studied them, realizing that they were the key to resolving Harrison's possible role in the murders.

They showed that Harrison had been going to Dr. Bell once and sometimes twice a week for years.

Marina left Harrison's with one thing on her mind. She needed a court order to get Harrison's medical information from Dr. Bell. She went back to the office and put the paperwork together.

It was getting late. Both Shepherd and Spaulding had gone home for the evening. Spaulding answered his private line and listened to her update. Afterward, he ordered her to go home and get some rest and leave the court order for the first thing in the morning.

Reluctantly, she stopped work for the day. At home, Marina received a call from Reed. He was still in a lot of pain. For some reason he'd decided to try to wean himself off the pain medication as soon as possible and it was taking a toll on him. This made talking to him and trying to maintain a degree of normalcy extremely difficult. She was actually glad to get off the phone. Lying in the dark, she fought waves of guilt and sadness. She should have been the one on the porch getting shot and the one in the hospital. Marina fell into an uneasy sleep.

With Reed out of the task force picture Marina doubled her efforts to finish the job. She got up early the next day and had her court order by ten in the morning. She was at Dr. Bell's downtown office requesting Harrison's medical records half an hour later.

Dr. Everett Bell was a thin, scholarly-looking man

who hid his big gray eyes behind black wire-rimmed glasses. He sat at his contemporary desk in his office doing paperwork while Marina went through Harrison's records. He'd agreed to answer general psychiatric questions, but could not give her specifics about his sessions with Harrison without Harrison's permission.

That said, he was concerned about his patient and planned to see Harrison to help him. Marina wanted to be one of the first to talk to Harrison if he came out of whatever state he was in.

She combed through the thick stack of medical files slowly, studying each page filled with Bell's angular scrawl. Harrison had something called Dissociative Identity Disorder. Having gone through a series of computer searches, she knew the term was used for people with multiple personalities.

In the notes from the early sessions, she read that Harrison had been a severely abused child. His mother had starved, beat and burned him. Dr. Bell wrote that he thought this was how the additional ego or person-ality, Harry, had been born. Harrison's aunt had gone to court to have him taken from his mother. His mother had served time in prison for child abuse.

Checking time periods, Marina skipped ahead to Harrison's college years. Dr. Bell had met Ava, another one of Harrison's personalities then. She had come out when Harrison had been pressured to participate in the fraternity parties that included rapes and assaults on female students.

Marina rubbed her forehead. This information forced more questions to surface. She wondered if Harrison had actually *participated* in any of the rapes and assaults. If he hadn't, why had he been accused by some of the victims? Then there was the question of Ava, one of his egos. With Harrison being dressed as a woman, it sounded as though Ava was the one who'd shot Reed and threatened to kill John. John said she'd acted as if he'd done something to her, like rape. Marina wondered if Harrison could have been assaulted and blanked it out of his memory.

Standing, she took several of the records to be copied. The serial avenger puzzle was making her head hurt.

As she prepared to leave, Marina got a call from one of the guys at the station. Harrison had been transferred to a state facility where they would try to determine if he was fit to stand trial for attempting to murder Reed and John. This was a lot less than murder charges for the Alpha Kappa Epsilon members who had been murdered, but until and unless she could tie Harrison to the other crimes there wasn't much she could do.

She told the doctor about Harrison's transfer. Then, hoping that Dr. Bell would be able to bring Harrison out of the state he was in, she followed him to the facility.

The state facility was in a small Illinois town west of Chicago. Tall, elegant-looking gates enclosed a modern-looking building surrounded by lushly sculptured grass, flowers and shrubs. If she hadn't known the place for what it was, she would have guessed an upscale private hospital. Glad that she and Dr. Bell had called ahead, Marina checked in at the gate, parked her car and went in the main entrance.

The facility director double-checked their paperwork and welcomed them. He told them that Harrison had been seen by one of their doctors. The doctor had failed to bring him out of the mental state, but hadn't given up yet. An assistant showed them to where Harrison was being kept.

Harrison was in a small room with a bed. The walls were sterile white. The door was heavy steel with a thick mesh-covered glass at eye level. Harrison sat on the bed, unmoving. His eyes were open but he stared ahead blankly.

Dr. Bell asked them to move Harrison to one of the consult or treatment rooms. The staff complied. Soon Marina was watching Dr. Bell with Harrison from the other side of a one-way mirror.

Bell spent a lot of time talking to Harrison and trying to make him feel comfortable. Listening from her vantage point, Marina found the ebb and flow of his voice hypnotic. Harrison wasn't reacting.

Bell continued to talk. He began to ask Harrison questions about how he felt. He focused on Harrison being safe from harm and with someone who cared about him.

Marina relaxed into her desk chair, abruptly aware of how tired she was. She hadn't slept much in the past few days. She saw Harrison sort of fall forward on the couch.

Suddenly much more alert, she heard Bell asking him if he was all right. Harrison was shaking. "I couldn't stop her," he mumbled.

Bell went to comfort him. "Harrison, you're all right now, but a crime has been committed—actually several. The authorities need to talk to you about it. Can you do that? It's very important."

Harrison nodded. "I couldn't stop her," he repeated.

Dr. Bell gave him water from a pitcher on the side table.

Marina got on her cell phone and asked Reed's C.P.D. buddy Marco to come down to assist in the interrogation. By the time he arrived, Harrison was somewhat calm. They read him his rights and turned on the tape.

"Did you drug John Stuart at your cabin?" Marina asked, starting the questions.

Harrison lifted his head, shaking it. "No, she did it. She wanted to make him pay."

Marina pressed him. "Who's she? What is her name?"

"Ava."

"The Ava who lives inside you?" Dr. Bell asked.

Harrison hung his head. "Yes."

"Why did she want to make John Stuart pay?" Marco inquired calmly.

"She…she says he raped her, that all of them did."

"Who is she accusing of rape, Harrison? What are their names?" Marina interjected, ignoring the tension bunching the muscles at the back of her neck.

"Aubrey Russell, Colton Edwards, Elliot Washington, Flint Huber and John Stuart."

Dr. Bell made eye contact with him. "Harrison, did you see them rape Ava?"

Harrison shook his head. "No. No, I blacked out."

Forcing more air into her lungs, Marina leaned forward. "Did you see Ava shoot Lieutenant Crawford?"

Harrison swallowed hard. "Yes, but I couldn't stop her. She was too strong for me."

"Did you see her hurt or kill anyone else?" Marco asked in a deceptively calm voice.

Harrison was trembling again. He hung his head. His words came out slow and halting. "Yes. She...killed the men who raped her."

"Which men?"

"Aubrey, Colton, Elliot and Flint."

Marina fisted one hand along the bottom of her chair. She had to be certain. "How did she kill them?"

Harrison looked at her like she was a dimwit. "Ava is beautiful and she loves disguises. She lured each man to a private place, drugged him and killed him."

"But *how* did she kill them?" Marina repeated.

"With a knife she stole from the Alpha Kappa Epsilon house. Then she castrated them. I—I tried, but I couldn't stop her."

Marina relaxed against the back of her chair in a sort of daze. They'd finally caught the serial avenger. She didn't know if the murdered men had actually raped Ava. She thought it was more likely that Ava had somehow identified with the group's victims so much that she imagined herself as one of them. The pertinent fact was that Ava thought she was a victim and had acted on that assertion.

"Ava, will you come out and talk to us, explain your

actions?" Dr. Bell prompted. "If Harrison gets prison time for this you are going to be there right along with him."

Everyone focused on Harrison, waiting for some sort of reaction. Marina was remembering the blonde she'd chased through the trail at the preserve and their fight at the end. She hadn't known it was Harrison, even when she'd ripped off the blond wig to find the brown hair beneath it.

Several moments passed. Dr. Bell sighed and stood. "I've talked to Ava a few times. She can hear and see everything Harrison can, but she'll only come out when she wants to," he explained.

Marina and Marco left the facility, anxious to have the tape transcribed and entered into evidence. Marco shook Marina's hand as she prepared to get into her car. "Congratulations. You and Reed did some good work on the task force," he said.

Marina thanked him. "I don't know if they're going to find Harrison competent to stand trial," she noted, "but the important thing is that we've stopped the murders and gotten him off the street."

Marco smiled approvingly. "That's right, focus on the positive. Word in the department is that if Reed can bring this one in successfully he'll get that promotion he's been looking for."

The thought made her lips curve upward. "I sure hope so."

Chapter 20

Marina got home early from work to cook dinner and do a last-minute cleanup at her place. Reed was coming over for the first time since he'd gotten out of the hospital. He'd been staying at his mother's for weeks while his wounds healed and it had been hard on Marina and him. Now, she could barely contain her excitement.

In the early days of his being back to work on half days, he'd talked a good game, but she'd seen the sheer exhaustion in his eyes and demeanor when she'd dropped by his mother's house after work. She hadn't been ready to risk a setback in his health and healing for a few nights of pleasure. She'd already been waiting for Reed Crawford for a while and knew that a few more weeks wouldn't break her.

Humming to herself, she checked the contents of her refrigerator for the umpteenth time. That's how many times she'd changed her mind on the menu. No matter how much she considered cooking steak or preparing a host of fancy recipes she'd copied off the Internet, the image of them lingering over a romantic spaghetti dinner stayed with her.

Removing the ingredients from her refrigerator and cabinets, she washed her hands and began to chop the vegetables. With the noodles done and sauce simmering, she escaped to her room to change.

The dress she'd chosen for tonight left no doubts as to her intentions. Reed has chosen it at the store where Jasmine worked. It was red, her favorite color. The halter top dipped low between her generous breasts and the dropped waist hugged her hips. She wore her hair down, adding light makeup and big earrings that framed her face. When the doorbell rang she stepped into rhinestone-studded mules.

Marina opened the door. Reed stood on her doorstep looking extra good in his blue suit. "Reed," she said, pure joy adding an extra lift to her voice, "you didn't have to wear a suit. It's just us for dinner."

He was staring at her dress so hard that heat rushed her face. "Seeing you and that dress, I'm glad I did." His voice took on a husky note. "You look like the present I always wanted but never got."

Widening the door opening and thanking him, she moved aside to let him in.

As soon as she closed the door he pulled her into a tight embrace. Up against his lean-muscled body and sculpted chest, her breath came out on a sigh. She closed her eyes. Being in his arms was heaven. It had been too long since they'd been alone together.

"I missed you," he whispered.

Her gaze locked with his. "I missed you, too."

For several moments they simply held each other, hugging and kissing.

"Are you hungry?" she asked, tearing herself away from him.

"Starving." The light in his eyes let her know that he wasn't just talking about food.

"The…the food's ready. I just have to finish the garlic bread and dish up the salad."

"Let me help you," he said, following her to the kitchen.

"Did you have a hard day at work?" she asked, bending to put the sliced bread in the oven.

"It was the usual."

Marina straightened. He was so busy staring her behind that he nearly spilled salad from one of the bowls.

Something curled deep in the pit of her stomach. "Would you like a glass of wine?"

"Sure." He busied himself pouring salad dressing.

Retrieving the open bottle of red wine she'd left breathing on the countertop, she filled two wineglasses and gave him one.

He accepted the glass, his hand massaging hers and moving up her arm. "What do we toast?"

Marina smiled. "Your good health? Your new promotion?"

"Yeah, I got the promotion and the doctor gave me a clean bill of health yesterday. I'm down for anything now."

"Anything?" she asked with a teasing lilt to her voice.

"Anything," he confirmed, pulling her closer.

She chuckled. "Then we should certainly drink to your health."

They toasted his health and stared at each other over the rims of their glasses. They moved closer, like opposite ends of a magnet, destined to meet. Their lips came together. She slipped her tongue inside to taste Reed and to touch her tongue to his. Tilting her head up, she leaned into him. They both sighed.

The buzzer on the stove went off.

"The b-bread," she stammered, looking for a pot holder. "I've got to take the bread out."

He nodded, watching her silently.

"I'll put the salads on the table," he said, lifting the bowls and exiting the kitchen.

At the stove, Marina found herself shaking. She swallowed more wine and worked on her breathing. The bread had browned beautifully, but she was no longer hungry, at least for food. She placed the garlic bread in a basket and set it on the table. Then she fixed plates of thin noodles covered in meat and vegetable sauce for Reed and herself and carried them to the dining area.

"Looks good and smells good," he remarked, looking

down at his plate. He glanced at the plate she'd fixed for herself. "Is that all you're going to eat?"

"I'm not that hungry," she explained. "I guess I'm just excited."

"I'm excited, too," he murmured, his brown eyes deepening. "I haven't been able to think of food since I saw you in that dress. Come here."

Reaching across the table he took her hand and tugged her toward him. Marina let him pull her down onto his lap. Their lips met in a voracious kiss. She tangled her fingers in his thick hair. Reed's mouth traced a path from her neck into the deep valley between her breasts left bare by the dress.

Reed whispered against her skin. "I want…I want…"

She lifted his chin with her fingers. "What do you want?"

His brown-eyed gaze burned into hers. "You, Marina. You're all I can think about."

She cupped his face in her hands. "I want you, too. I've been dreaming it for weeks."

Placing her feet on the floor, he stood, taking her hand.

"This way," she said, leading him to her bedroom.

Inside, she pulled back the sheets and stepped out of her mules.

Reed shrugged out of his suit coat and placed his tie on the nightstand. Marina helped him hurry through the buttons on his shirt. With it open, she pressed her lips to the warm caramel skin on his chest and playfully tongued a nipple. She felt him tense and heard his quick intake of breath. Looking at him, touching his toned and fit body, made her that much more excited. She pushed the shirt off his wide shoulders.

"Marina." He moved his hands down her sides, curving them around to squeeze her buttocks. She pressed herself against the hard heat of his body. Pulling her into his arms, he slid down the zipper on her dress. The soft red silk fell from her like skin on an exotic fruit. With a groan, he placed her on the bed and covered every inch of her bare skin with his hot mouth. Moaning and shaking beneath his passionate assault, she felt Reed hook his fingers in the sides of her red lace panties and slide them down and off. She sat up and helped him remove his pants and boxers and pull on a condom.

They came together, touching, feeling and kissing. She locked gazes with Reed, her mouth falling open as he pushed into her. She hooked her legs around his waist. He covered her mouth, nibbling her lips and sliding his tongue against hers as he moved in and out of her, hard and hot.

Shoving her hips upward, she felt him go deep. She rocked with him in a wild and funky rhythm that kept them both breathless and panting. At the peak, they held each other tight, tumbling forward in a free-fall rush to earth.

Afterward they lay together, hot and sweaty and satisfied. Reed tucked her into the curve of his body and put his mouth close to her ear to whisper, *"Querida Marina. Estoy enamorado de ti."*

Marina's lids opened. "W-what did you say?"

He repeated the phrase.

She smiled and snuggled closer. "I'm in love with you, too. You've been taking Spanish lessons?"

He gently nibbled on her ear. "Javier's been helping me out to sort of make up for backing the wrong guy last time."

"Whoo, my dad is full of surprises," she exclaimed. "And so are you."

Reed's mouth burned a path down her neck to linger on her breasts. "Javier's determined to make sure I feel welcome in the family."

She gasped softly. "Oh, you are *so* welcome in the family. Next you'll be telling me that we're going to work another task force together."

"Well, I was saving that for later…"

"What?" Her lids lifted as she reached for him.

He moved down to tongue her navel.

Her breath came out in a rush as he nipped her waist and continued down the length of her leg. "Reed?" she gasped.

"New FBI and C.P.D. task force," he murmured against her skin on his way back up. "We'll talk about it later. Did I ever tell you what gorgeous legs you have?"

"Reed!" Marina threaded her fingers through his hair, moving them down to massage his powerful shoulders as he lifted her leg and began to thrust into her again. She couldn't think with him moving inside her like that, but she'd get the details later.

* * * * *

Read on for a sneak preview of
Eternally *by Maureen Child,*
the first exciting instalment of
THE GUARDIANS *mini-series, available*
exclusively from Mills & Boon® Intrigue,
NOCTURNE *in June 2008!*

Eternally

by

Maureen Child

Kieran MacIntyre felt the fire still burning his fingertips and a part of him stood back and wondered at it. Through the countless centuries he'd been wandering this earth, he'd never experienced that jolt. He'd known others of his kind who had and in the beginning, he'd even been jealous of it.

But as time passed and the years piled up behind him like dirty beads on a piece of string, he'd learned that he was the lucky one. He had no distractions to keep him from the hunt. He had no other to worry about. He didn't have to concern himself with agonizing over the loss of a Mate when he'd never found one.

Until now.

He'd first become aware of her three months ago when she'd called his home trying to set up an interview with him. Naturally her request was rejected, but he'd looked her up online and had been immediately intrigued. Her photo had haunted him since and he'd made it his business to keep a distant eye on her. Until tonight of course, when he'd been forced to confront her.

Stray curls of dark red hair escaped from the ridiculous ponytail she wore at the top of her head. Her green eyes were huge in a pale face sprinkled with just a few golden freckles. Instinct pushed at him to grab her. Hold her. Tip her head back, taste her neck, feel her pulse pound beneath his mouth. Fill his hands with her breasts and bury himself in her heat.

His body roared with life and a hunger he'd never known before. And he didn't want it. Didn't need it. He'd survived for this long without a Mate and he'd done a hell of a job of it, too. He'd never liked complications. Not in life and certainly not since his death. Easier by far to keep his distance from the mortal world, do his job and then fade from the memory of everyone whose life he'd touched.

Better to be alone.

Count on no one but himself and the other Guardians.

But she smelled sweet. Fresh.

Alive.

The floral shampoo she used clung to her seductively and he wondered if her skin would taste as good as she smelled. Her high, full breasts rose and fell quickly with her agitated breathing and her eyes seemed to get bigger, wider, as she watched him.

Did she sense the connection between them?

Could she have any idea at all about what was to come?

"Who are you?" she asked quietly, her whisper almost swallowed by the noise drifting to them from the adjacent room.

Who was he? An interesting question. Guardian? Warrior? Knight? Too many answers and not enough time.

He took a step closer, and she moved too, backing up until she bumped into the kitchen counter behind her. She jolted in surprise and dropped the carton of ice cream to the floor.

She couldn't know. Couldn't even imagine the world he moved through.

His gaze locked with hers, Kieran moved in even closer, dipping his head, letting her fill him with scents that drugged him, that poured through him like rich wine.

His heartbeat thundered in his chest.

He had no time for this. And yet, he knew he couldn't leave her without one taste. Since he first saw her photo, he'd known this moment would come—now, he wouldn't waste it. Cupping her cheeks between his palms, he took her mouth, intending only a brief, hard kiss that would assuage the sudden, all-encompassing need raging within. But one brush of her lips to his and he was lost.

She sighed into his mouth and her lips opened for him. His tongue swept into her depths and he felt himself drowning in the heat of her. Senses overloading, his body felt engulfed in flames. She sighed again and the soft sound spiraled through him like knives, tearing through a centuries old apathy as if it were fragile silk.

Her breasts pressed to his chest, he felt the thundering beat of her heart as if it were his own. It shuddered through him, pounding in his head, his blood.

She dropped the spoon and it clattered on the tile floor like a warning bell.

Kieran groaned, let her go and reluctantly stepped away, willing his body into quiet. The instinct to take her was strong, nearly overpowering. She trembled, eyes wide, and he wanted to lay her down on the floor and lose himself in the heat of her.

"Wow," she said softly, "you're really good at that."

He rubbed one hand across his mouth and refused to admit he was shaking. He had no time for this. No time to be distracted by something he wasn't going to claim anyway.

He wasn't here for her.

Exactly.

Kieran had followed the scent of his prey to this house. All day, he'd hunted it, always a step or two behind. Tracking the elusive trace energy signature all demons left in their wake. Now, it seemed that Fate had taken a turn in the hunt. Why else would the beast he sought have come here?

To *her* house?

The power of the beast throbbed in the air, its hunger, its desire pulsing wildly and it amazed Kieran anew that the mortals couldn't sense it. Somewhere in this house, the demon moved freely, already on the hunt, deciding who it would kill and when.

And he was the only man who could stop it.

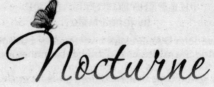

Celebrate 100 years of pure reading pleasure with Mills & Boon®

To mark our centenary, each month we're publishing a special 100th Birthday Edition. These celebratory editions are packed with extra features and include a FREE bonus story.

Plus, starting in February you'll have the chance to enter a fabulous monthly prize draw. See 100th Birthday Edition books for details.

Now that's worth celebrating!

15th February 2008

Raintree: Inferno by Linda Howard
Includes FREE bonus story Loving Evangeline
A double dose of Linda Howard's heady mix of passion and adventure

4th April 2008

The Guardian's Forbidden Mistress by Miranda Lee
Includes FREE bonus story The Magnate's Mistress
Two glamorous and sensual reads from favourite author Miranda Lee!

2nd May 2008

The Last Rake in London by Nicola Cornick
Includes FREE bonus story The Notorious Lord
Lose yourself in two tales of high society and rakish seduction!

Look for Mills & Boon 100th Birthday Editions at your favourite bookseller or visit www.millsandboon.co.uk

FREE

4 BOOKS AND A SURPRISE GIFT!

We would like to take this opportunity to thank you for reading this Mills & Boon® book by offering you the chance to take FOUR more specially selected titles from the Intrigue series absolutely FREE! We're also making this offer to introduce you to the benefits of the Mills & Boon® Reader Service™—

- ★ **FREE home delivery**
- ★ **FREE gifts and competitions**
- ★ **FREE monthly Newsletter**
- ★ **Books available before they're in the shops**
- ★ **Exclusive Reader Service offers**

Accepting these FREE books and gift places you under no obligation to buy; you may cancel at any time, even after receiving your free shipment. Simply complete your details below and return the entire page to the address below. You don't even need a stamp!

YES! Please send me 4 free Intrigue books and a surprise gift. I understand that unless you hear from me, I will receive 6 superb new titles every month for just £3.15 each, postage and packing free. I am under no obligation to purchase any books and may cancel my subscription at any time. The free books and gift will be mine to keep in any case.

I8ZEE

Ms/Mrs/Miss/Mr.............................Initials ....
BLOCK CAPITALS PLEASE

Surname ....

Address ....

....

....Postcode ....

Send this whole page to:
The Reader Service, FREEPOST CN81, Croydon, CR9 3WZ